TWENTY OF THEIR SWORDS

BY

HOLMES M. ALEXANDER

PHILADELPHIA

DORRANCE & COMPANY

To
My Father and Mother
And
The Memory of My Sister.

*"Alack there lies more peril in thine eye
Than twenty of their swords."*

Romeo and Juliet.
Act II—Scene 2.

I

Davis Pettigrier opened one eye and twisted his head
just enough to see into the pew diagonally adjacent to
the one in which he and his father and mother were
bowed in prayer. It was not the first time that he had
permitted this pew to distract his attention from the
service. The new family that occupied it had moved
to Cranston two months before and for several Sundays had been under his observation. Today Davis
had heard his father tell Mrs. Pettigrier that the
Lucases had become members. With an effort and a
stab of remorse Davis recalled his attention to the
service. Mechanically he followed the responses to
the Litany. "Save us, Good Lord." "Good Lord,
deliver us."

The Litany was over. "Let us pray," suggested
Dr. Peckam. He prayed and the people said "Amen."
There was a scraping of leather on wood as the kneel-
ing ones and those pretending to kneel settled back
into their seats. Davis took the opportunity created
by this mild disturbance. Now the object of his scrutiny was better revealed. He could see a pink and
white profile, a cluster of brown, wispy curls. They
were spirals that made you want to run your finger
inside.

Dr. Peckam, five feet six, towered from the pulpit
and bent to his favorite text: "Ye are of more worth
than any sparrows." During the first half Davis sat
following, as best he could, the argument. He enjoyed
a snug courage in hearing that God would not suffer
a righteous man to caste his foot against a stone.
There was really nothing to fear in life, thought the
boy, as long as you were pious, virtuous and sincere.

But when Dr. Peckam went on and began to deal with illustrations and allusions less graphic than feet and stones, Davis' thoughts wandered, and soon his eyes followed his thoughts as far as the neighboring pew.

"Nice chap, Lucas," said Mr. Pettigrier when they all three were homeward bound in his expensive limousine. "My father and his were neighbors down here, but Lucas moved to Boston and I never knew him well. Made his money in Grafton Chemicals during the war."

Sunday dinner was an occasion. Seldom if ever did the Pettigrier family sit down alone. Alvin Martin, attorney-at-law, a testy bachelor of forty who had one shoulder an inch lower than the other from a hunting accident years ago, was a permanent Sunday guest, although his chair had been empty for three years during the War. He was a hero to Davis, for in 1915 Martin had gone to France as a private citizen and enlisted as a *poilu*. He had resumed his place less than a year ago. On this particular Sunday Martin was not the only guest, for the Louis Davises, Mrs. Pettigrier's brother and his wife, were there.

At the table they talked of President Wilson's Fourteen Points and the Versailles conference.

Alvin Martin said, "Those Europeans are like prize-fighters; they don't fight for nothing or for anything as abstract as a cause. Germany'll be bled just as France was in '71. England got her colonies, France, money and land, and Italy too. What's more, they haven't paid for their victory yet. Wait till the British and French men come home and try to get their jobs back. Why, they'll starve in the streets."

"Oh, Alvin," said Mrs. Davis. "Do you mean to say this is just like all other wars? I thought this was to make the world safe for democracy. Wasn't that the reason you were so anxious to get into it?"

"I was anxious to get in for the same reason I ride races with this shoulder. I like to be scared. It gives me a big thrill. The sooner people get rid of this propaganda that the Allies all went in to chain the wild beast of nations, the better it's going to be. Then at least we can have some intelligent voters."

"Don't mind old Alvin," said the host. "He's getting along, and he likes to be cynical. Next he'll be saying that Germany didn't start the war."

"I'm likely to say France and Russia had as much to do with it as Germany did. As a matter of fact—"

"Well," Mrs. Pettigrier hastened to avert an argument, "you men better fight it all out after dinner. How was your tennis this morning, Alvin?"

"Rotten! How was the sermon?"

"You should come some time and judge for yourself."

"I'd rather sit home and knit than hear one of those well-fed hypocrites get up and gas."

"Wow!" said Mr. Davis. "Someone's been feeding you raw meat. You must have had a bad morning."

"More likely a bad night, eh Alvin?" This last from Mr. Pettigrier.

There were times—and this was one of them—when Davis was not sure that he liked Alvin Martin. Alvin was forever casting stones at his hot house of ideals. Davis could not possibly think of Germany as anything but a land of demons or of a clergyman as anything but a man of ordained goodness; not that he knew any Germans, or that he really knew any ministers, but simply that he had been told certain things and that he believed them. Such tirades as Alvin's set him thinking, and it was a painful process to have rational thought thundering at the walls of conventional idealism. Even in the older man's estimate of himself Davis felt a tinge of discomfort. He wanted to believe Alvin was a gallant crusader, and in spite of everything he would believe it.

That evening his neighbor, Tom Stevenson, came. "You're not going to back out now, Dave?"

"No," said Davis. "I'll get my coat."

The distance from the Pettigriers' country home to Cranston could be diminished by a short cut which led down an unfinished dirt road and across a set of railroad tracks. The crossing here was blind, but the road was so little used that there was neither watchman nor bell. Tom and Davis always took this way to school or to their friends' homes in town. Experience had taught them that only two fast trains ran past there a day, the six fifty-five in the morning and the six ten in the evening. On Sundays there were none, and so this Sunday they bumped over the tracks with scarcely a break in the conversation.

"I've never done anything like this before, Tom. Do I look all right?"

"You look fine," Tom said without turning his eyes.

They stopped before a large house, and Tom rang John Lucas' door-bell.

"Don't forget, Tom, you promised to go whenever I give the high sign."

Davis hesitated on the threshold of the living-room. The room was full of people. He felt that every one was staring at him, laughing at his embarrassment. He crimsoned with chagrin and shame.

"Oh, I'm so glad to see you. *Do* come in and sit down." Davis gulped awkwardly and took the proffered hand. He was annoyed that his own was wet and hot. He found himself the most inconspicuous seat, a footstool, which happened to be next the fire. Margie Lucas sat down on the sofa, and Tom quickly took the seat beside her. For a few minutes Davis found himself obscured by the lively talk carried on by the others, then the young hostess made an attempt to bring him into it.

"Oh, wasn't that a wonderful sermon of Dr. Peckam's today?" she asked, looking across at him.

"Yes, I thought it was wonderful. I thought it—" Without warning Margie jumped up and went toward the door. "Oh, I'm so glad to see you. Do come in and sit down." Two other Sunday regulars filed in, and Davis had to move closer to the fire to make room.

For some seconds, a polite hush hung over the company, and then Margie looked at Davis again. "Excuse me for interrupting," she said sweetly. "What were you saying?"

"Oh, I said it was wonderful."

After that he sat unmolested. He shot languishing, hidden glances at the goddess who held court in the room, but not once did he attempt to utter a word. Meanwhile, the fire became hotter. His left leg and side suffered torment. There were no other seats in the room except a footstool at her feet. To stand up would turn everyone's attention on him and he would be begged to sit down. He tried to catch Tom's eye, but Tom's eyes were both engaged. By a subtle movement he twisted his burning leg and side a little out of the way and exposed his back. For a while this afforded relief but not for long. Soon he was in agony again. He dared not resume his former position because now his legs were under a chair and could not be removed without disturbing the occupant. Two more visitors arrived. They looked about for seats and Davis, clutching at the chance, said, "Here, take mine." But one of the newcomers squeezed in beside Margie and Tom on the sofa, and the other took the only remaining position, the one at her feet.

This interruption gave Davis a chance to rise and enjoy a short respite, but his torments were redoubled when the butler appeared with a fresh log. The added fuel made his situation absolutely unbearable. In the courage of despair he asked the boy next to him to prod Tom. Tom, prodded, looked toward his friend and saw the "high sign." He telegraphed back a protest, but Davis indicated his determination, and soon they took a lingering farewell.

They drove home together, and it was a very silent twelve miles. Davis was busy with new and disturbing thoughts, and Tom respected his silence. Two less devoted companions would have wearied each other with forced conversation, but Davis stepped out of the car at his own house with "Thanks, Tom. See you to-morrow." That was all.

II

Monday morning dawned with all the portents of
another school week. Davis was awakened by his
father's familiar bellow up the stairs (for Davis had
the third floor all to himself) and opened unwilling
eyes on a world drenched and darkened by a cold down-
pour. For a minute or so he "played possum" but the
insistent "Davis, get up right away! Davis, do you
hear? Are you up yet?" finally broke his morale. He
answered, "Yes, Father," and dropped his feet to the
cold floor. For a few minutes on Monday mornings
Davis was not at all sure that he loved his father as he
should. In fact, during the brief period it took him
to find his slippers and rush to the comparative warmth
of the bathroom, filial affection was distinctly on the
ebb. By the time, however, that he had dressed,
packed his bag in preparation for the purgatorial week
ahead and descended to the dining-room, all such re-
bellious emotions had been dissipated or were soon to
be, in cereal and cream, eggs and bacon. And when
the father extracted, as he always did, from his morning paper, the sport sheet and passed it to the boy,
devotion resumed once more its high level.

Davis Pettigrier was at this time sixteen. Physically
he seemed undeveloped. He was tall, and his spindle
legs appeared hardly strong enough to support the frail
body. Were it not for a seemingly misplaced look of
virility in the eyes, his pale face might have been that
of a rather plain girl.

Perhaps his emotions were by nature pitched higher
than those of his contemporaries, or, what is more
probable, they had been subjected to greater stimuli;

11

but whatever the reason, the fact remained that the relationship between father and son was unusual. Few boys of his age have an aggressive and individual affection for their parents. What they have is either a sentimental and superimposed idea that it is their bounden duty to love their parents, or else a half-rebellious fear that results in sulky obedience and, often, deceit. Davis Pettigrier was not tied by such bonds. There was an affinity between them that made Davis capable of understanding the old pride which so often flashed behind the troubled eyes or expressed itself in an impatient twist of the tired shoulders. Perhaps it was the same glint in his own eyes and the same set of his shoulders which made people say that he "took after" his father. Perhaps these had something to do with the tacit bond between them, but to Davis there was a less abstract explanation.

He remembered one Christmas day when he and his little brother and sister stopped on the threshold of their living room with "ohs" of delight, for there under the Christmas tree stood a Shetland pony hitched to a basket cart. He remembered the happy days that followed. At first, Mr. Pettigrier insisted that an older person be with them when they went driving in the cart. Sometimes it was himself or their mother, often Mac, the black gardener who was never slow to lay aside either his pipe or his hoe to join them.

One day in March Davis had his tenth birthday, and when his father told him that he was now a little man Davis claimed, on the strength of this new development, the guardianship of the cart.

He had been told not to go off the place and he had not meant to, but there was only one good place to trot, down the driveway that led to the main road. Surely, said his brother, Daddy wouldn't mind if they crossed the road to turn around.

Of course, he had no recollection of how that Saturday afternoon when Mr. and Mrs. Pettigrier were arranging some new books in the library a rattling car pulled up at the front door and three men carried in three dirty bundles, only one of which was breathing. All that Davis remembered of the consequences was that he lay in a dark room stiff with bandages and that he saw a huge monster that roared at him and pounced on him and screamed like little Nancy and Bobby. He remembered that he continued to see this monster long after he got well, but that he never saw Nancy and Bobby again. He remembered, rather to his shame, that for months he would not sleep alone, he would not go into a dark room, or even down to the stable in daylight, for fear of the monster. And through it all he remembered a big hand in his own that never let go, a deep, heartening voice that never rebuked him and a bent shoulder and rough cheek he could lay his head against and weep.

He was two years coming out of the valley of terror, and when he emerged he found himself a stranger in a strange world. But the one who had led him out was still with him. It was this one who tossed a baseball or football with him, who taught him to ride a pony, who took him and his friends to the circus and who helped him with his lessons at night until finally the stranger began to learn the ways of the strange world, dared to let loose the big hand and to walk alone.

Only when he had walked alone for a while did Davis become conscious of the bonds that tightened on his heart. Youth takes much for granted, and it may have been that the first time he became aware of these bonds was only eighteen months ago when his father lay stricken with pneumonia and the doctors took Davis aside and told him he must be very brave. After that the boy began to look into the face of the person whose hand he had clung to and to read there a tale of suffering and noble devotion that made him very solemn.

III

Barclay School on Monday mornings was a hotbed of rebellion and resignation. It was a state of affairs best expressing the attitude of:

"Ten thousand times I've done my best
And all's to do again."

There was young Phil Parsons, slim, handsome and worldly wise, with a nervous eye and a restless hand. He rebelled. Phil hated the school and loathed the work. He meant to take it out on his oppressors. It was he who tossed a lighted fire cracker into "Bull" Bennett's geometry class and he, also, who blew out all the fuses in the building one night and started the big riot. For both offenses he escaped unscathed. He was bold in his schemes, brilliant in his studies, and the faculty feared him. And there was good-natured Tom Stevenson, stupid as an ox and hopelessly browbeaten. Tom never got into disciplinary trouble. He worked too hard, shaking his shaggy head and damning his own stupidity over a bit of Shakespeare or a chemical formula. And huge, clumsy Joe Watson, "Short Cut" Watson they called him, who never did his work till he had the consensus of opinion on the easiest method. He bent his neck meekly to the yoke and only grunted a protest when the scourge was applied.

These were Davis Pettigrier's best friends. Davis and Phil were roommates, and Tom and Joe. Their names grouped together among their colleagues as naturally as "Barnum and Bailey." "Davis 'n Phil," you would hear people say, or "Joe 'n Tom."

Barclay School did not take cognizance of the state

of its pupils' hearts. Like Nature's winds which blow upon the cloaked and uncloaked, it used the absolute standard. When Davis returned from his week-end at home his struggles for concentration were lethargic. He found himself leaning on his elbows over an open book with his mind vagrant. His masters threatened and stormed. They predicted failure.

One night, the eve of an important test, Davis went to his room and prayed. He prayed for strength, for power, for knowledge. Might he only remember his theorems tomorrow. Might he only draw his figures correctly. He rose, turned on the light and began to undress. Phil was in another room working. Phil never prayed, and he never failed. Davis remembered that he, himself, had prayed and failed before. Thoughtfully he slipped back into his coat and vest. He sought the room where Phil was studying.

"Do you mind if I work here, Phil? You're a good example."

If Davis lacked energy and enthusiasm in the formal pursuit of knowledge, it may have been because he squandered these qualities in the pursuit of athletic glory. Yet, in spite of his difference in attitude, one pursuit was as vain as the other. No amount of aggressive determination could overcome his natural handicap. His most frantic efforts on the football field proved unavailing, and it was only the inevitable that happened when he was released from the squad. Davis, although he was unfamiliar with the phrase, experienced the mature knowledge of the futility of human effort.

"The harder you try, the harder you fall," he told his roommate that night. But Phil was doing the Latin.

Davis sat disconsolate on the bed. Tom Stevenson entered the room.

"Finished with that book yet, Phil?"

"Almost."

Tom sat down beside Davis.

"Hear you were cut today, Dave."

There was nothing offensive in the way Tom said it; but Davis, in a particularly malicious humour, answered sourly, "Don't rub it in."

Tom looked hurt but remained silent. Phil evidently finished the task at hand, and, turning from the table where he was working, he tossed a book at Tom. It hit the edge of the bed and bounced off, falling at Davis' feet.

"What's that?" He picked it up, but Tom snatched it from him.

"None of your business." Davis jumped to the door and stood before it.

"Let me see it, Tom. I think I know what it is, but maybe I'm wrong. I hope so."

"Get out of my way before I knock you out." Tom held the book behind his back with one hand and pushed Davis aside with the other.

"All right then, I know what it is. It's a Latin trot. Lord, Tom, I never thought it of you." He had stepped away from the door and slumped down on the edge of the bed.

Tom also turned from the door. "Look here, Dave, I never did it before this fall, but I just couldn't keep up with all this football and everything. I had to use a trot. What's wrong with it anyhow?"

"You know what's wrong with it, all right. It's against the Honor System, and you know it."

Until now Phil had been silent, but at that he jumped up and whirled on his roommate. "I suppose you're going to tell, you damn Christer. Well, go on and get us fired if you want. Go ahead."

"I'm not going to tell. I've got nothing to say except that you-all ought to be ashamed of yourselves.

I never thought people did things like that, especially fellows I know."

Somebody turned the knob, and Davis pushed the accusing book under his pillow. It was Joe Watson. "What's the funeral?" he asked, looking about him at the unusual solemnity.

"Nothing at all," Davis tried to break the spell. "I just was kicking because I got cut."

"That's tough, Dave, but you'll make it next year. Say, Tom, did you get it?"

Tom reached under the pillow and produced the book. "Keep it, Joe; I don't want it. I'm going to do it alone."

Joe accepted it, shrugging his shoulders, walked out.

"I'll give you a lift with the Latin, Tom," said Davis. "I've already done mine." But Tom shut the door behind him without a word.

Time healeth all wounds, but the scar made by the discovery that his three best friends were doing something dishonest, or, at least, dishonorable, was deep, and it festered a long while under the surface. Rooming with Phil became more difficult every day. Both were now super-sensitive to each other's faults. When Phil insisted on playing the gramophone, Davis, instead of acquiescing as he used to, protested. And when Davis tied the lamp over his bed so as to read lying down, Phil complained that it shone in his eyes.

Joe often came into the room with the evident purpose of belittling the affair. Joe always laughed at Phil's jibes. He would throw back his big huge head and roar every time Phil called Davis a "cross-climber." Tom and Davis mutually avoided each other.

The football team continued a successful season, and Tom Stevenson became its outstanding figure. The week preceding the final game was one of tenseness at Barclay School. The State championship hung in the balance. On Wednesday night of that week Davis

was studying history. There was to be a test next
Tuesday. Reading of how Napoleon walked among
the soldiers on the eve of Austerlitz, Davis vaguely
thought how little it all mattered who won or lost
battles. He thought of the coming battle on Saturday.
Friday there would be a mass-meeting where the coach
and captain would speak. The coach would say the
team was "going out there and give all they had for
Barclay" and exhort the student body to do the same.
Then the captain would say so, too, and perhaps the
crowd would yell for Stevenson, and Tom would re-
iterate it all. If they won there would be a bonfire
Monday night and more speeches. If they lost there
would be no bonfire, but, whatever happened, Tuesday
there would be the history test.

It sounded foolish, Davis thought, but in his heart
he knew it would not seem foolish when it happened.
He knew that he would thrill to see the team run out
on the field and that he would cheer his heart away.
He scratched a note on the margin of the page—
"Austerlitz 1805. Napoleon vs. Austria and Russia."

Phil banged the door against the wall as he opened
it. Joe followed him in. "Still up on the cross. Let's
have a little come-to-Jesus meeting." Joe guffawed.
Davis shut his book and prepared to leave the room.
He had learned that it was best to clear out when Phil
was in a high humour.

While Davis gathered up his books Phil continued
his harangue inspired by Joe's appreciation. "Aw,
you cross-climbing hypocrite, think you're too good to
be in the room with us, don't you?"

"Yes."

"Here, take these books off my side the table."
Phil swept three books and a pad of paper to the floor.
It was the necessary straw. Davis plunged at him with
flying fists.

Phil, rallying from the first onslaught, drove his

opponent to the far wall with a mad rush. They clinched and rolled over and over on the floor, emitting smothered gasps and growls. Where God, who is said to be always with the strongest battalions, would have sided must remain forever a secret for His wisdom to disclose; for at that moment Tom Stevenson opened the door and, calling to Joe for assistance, fell to disentangling the combatants.

There was a short, sharp period of intervention, and, soon, Joe stood at one side of the room clasping Phil about the arms and body, while on the other side Tom had pinioned Davis.

"Let him alone, Phil," Joe was saying. "Finish down behind the gym, if you want, but not here."

"Damn right I'll finish it."

Joe loosened his hold to allow his principal to dab his nose with a handkerchief. Tom, noting his roommate's success, tried his own power of persuasion. "Don't make a fool of yourself, Dave. Cut it out."

But Davis' passion which had been longer in kindling was not so quickly cooled. "You damn cheat," he cried. "I hate you!" He tore himself loose and whirled on his erstwhile captor.

There were no flying fists, no parried jabs; the infuriated boy, transformed for the instant into an infuriated beast, flew straight at his enemy's throat. Ordinarily Tom, bigger, stronger and more active, could have brushed him off or felled him with one well-placed blow, but now the smaller animal bore him to the floor between the bed and the wall, where there was small room to struggle.

Joe and Phil, so lately captor and captive, now, with the alacrity of small and large nations, became allies and hastened to disengage the new combatants.

They were about this business when a new actor appeared in the person of one Mr. Ripple, who, being "dummy" of the bridge game in the masters' smoking-room, had come to investigate the commotion.

Mr. Ripple immediately asserted his authority and, waving Joe and Phil aside with an imperious gesture, seized Davis by the collar and dragged him forth.

"Rank disorder, Pettigrier. I shall have to report this to Dr. MacDonald. What does it mean?'"

By this time poor Davis' faculties were as dishevelled as his clothes; and his discretion had long ago gushed forth with his passion. He again turned his anger on the nearest object which happened, this time, to be Mr. Ripple. "Oh, go to hell, you damn fool! Let me loose." He began to struggle and, in the process, bestowed a few kicks on Mr. Ripple's shins. But Davis soon exhausted what little remained of his strength. A few shakes established his captor's superiority, and a *pax Romana* was enforced.

"I'll report you for insolence, too, Pettigrier. You're forgetting yourself. Stop, be still."

By this time a large audience had gathered and was enjoying the spectacle heartily. Having reasserted his prestige by a number of short speeches, Mr. Ripple marched his still defiant prisoner to the privacy of his own room where he endeavoured, for curiosity's sake, to find out the cause of the disturbance. Davis, however, proved sulky and silent, and in the end Mr. Ripple sent him to an empty room for the night and returned to the smoking-room where the bridge game was forgot in the rehearsal of his stirring adventures in the corridor.

The next morning Davis ignored the rising bell. He wished to avoid meeting his fellows in the showers, at breakfast and at chapel. At half-past nine the school bell boy knocked on the door and said that Doctor Mac-Donald would like to see him in the office.

"Davis," said the headmaster not unkindly, "what's all this. Mr. Ripple tells me he found three boys trying

to control you. He says you fought against him, swore
at him and were insolent. This is all new in you.
What's it all mean?"

Doctor MacDonald was prompted by more than
curiosity to delve into the cause of the boy's unprecedented behaviour. In the first place the Doctor liked
boys and thought he understood them, and in the
second he was a personal friend of Mr. Pettigrier.

Davis knew he was open to serious punishment. He
knew also that if he went back to the source of the
rupture with his friends, his actions would take on
a shade of virtue and that punishment, if it were not
entirely omitted, would be mitigated. Also, he knew
that if he exposed the matter of the "trot" Tom, Joe
and Phil would be liable even to expulsion.

"I've 'phoned your father," the headmaster went on.
"He'll be here soon. This is going to be pretty hard
on him, you know, unless you can explain. Sit down,
Davis."

Davis sat down and kept on thinking. No reason
to make a martyr of himself for those fellows. They
hadn't treated him squarely at all. He didn't owe them
a thing. If it were only himself there might be some
argument, but his father would suffer as much as anybody—probably more. And his mother. Somehow
Davis felt that his mother would not feel it as strongly
as his father, although she would weep. Davis sighed.
It was too much for him. Whatever he did would be
bad enough.

There was a knock at the door, and Tom Stevenson
answered the "Come in." "Could I speak to you a few
minutes, Doctor? It's about Dave—Dave's trouble."

"Doctor," Davis was out of his chair and between
the two. "Don't listen to him. Please, let me talk
to Tom first."

The headmaster searched back through his experience for precedent to cover such a case, but he found

none. He hesitated. Obviously, Pettigrier was going to silence some testimony Stevenson had to give. From the circumstances it appeared that Pettigrier had everything to gain and nothing to lose by new evidence. "You boys go back in the study, and when I send for you I want some explanation for all this nonsense."

Tom sat in the window-sill of the study and Davis on the desk. "Dave, I'm going to tell the whole story, as far as I'm concerned. It all started over that trot. I knew you wouldn't tell, yourself, even though Phil said you would."

Both were undergoing the usual struggle that boys put up against the show of emotion. Davis looked at the bookshelves and said, "I'm up for sassing old Ripple. This hasn't anything to do with the trot. Won't do anybody any good, only get yourself in trouble."

"It'll get you off a lot easier. You might get fired, you know, cussing at a master like that."

"He won't fire me, Tom. He and the old man are mighty thick. I'll get a week or so."

"That's bad enough. No, I'm sorry about the whole thing. I'm awful dumb, you know, and I found I couldn't stay up late working and then play decent football, so I started using Phil's trot. I'll never do it again, but I'm going to tell Mac the whole thing."

"How about Saturday? Who's going to take your place? Look, Tom." He pointed out the window behind Tom where they could see workmen putting up temporary wooden stands to take care of the expected crowd Saturday.

Tom looked wistful, and Davis felt a wave of emotion sweep over him. He forgot what he had been thinking last night about Austerlitz and battle. Of course, it mattered who won the game. Here was a chance to do a supreme service to his school. It was all the more supreme because it would be unselfish and unsung. He told Tom so.

"And I know if Father knew he would say I was right. But I won't tell that you—"

"That I cheated, you mean."

"Well, anyhow," Davis avoided the word, "it's all settled."

There was no handshaking or shoulder-slapping. Neither boy said another word, but within both was the realization that the old relationship existed again and that the old bond which had never been severed, but only tested, was reinforced now with triple brass.

When Davis went back to the office his father was there. "There's nothing to tell, Doctor MacDonald; I lost my temper and that's all. Tom wanted to say that he was fighting too, but I told him I was up for my trouble with Mr. Ripple, and that hadn't anything to do with him."

In the end he received a week's suspension.

That Saturday Davis parked his car a block or so away and walked to the game. He took a place at the end of the field where a crowd of chauffeurs and non-partisans sat on wooden benches. He heard the songs of the student body; he saw the team trot out, prancing like a high-strung horse before the plaudits of the crowd.

He looked yearningly at the cheering section. All bitterness about his release from the squad and his suspension were gone. He felt that every cheer belonged partly to him. No man on the field could do more for the school than he had done by making it possible for Tom to play.

The game began, and from the first whistle, as the Sunday papers had it, no one could say whether it was Barclay's day or Oakland's but it was certainly Tom Stevenson's. And because it was Tom's it was Barclay's in the end. After the game there was a snake dance, and the players were carried around the field. Tom Stevenson looked at the setting sun from the shoulders of his friends, and Davis Pettigrier saw it from the end of the field where the chauffeurs sat. They were both proud of themselves and of each other.

IV

Alvin Martin lived at the City Club. He had an
office down town and the reputation of being the
smartest lawyer in Cranston. People liked his cryptic
manner from a business point of view, but many were
hurt by his brusqueness in social intercourse. Old
ladies were horrified by his professed atheism and
young ones by his total indifference to their charms.
Men were often disconcerted to have their conversa-
tions punctuated by his snorts of contempt for their
opinions. He could never be counted upon to do or
say the conventional thing. He was always likely to
come to fashionable parties improperly dressed or to
tell his hostess that the soup was burnt. It had been
twenty years since he had answered an invitation in
writing. Yet Alvin Martin was never left off the
invitation list. He was a fixture in the social world,
because he came of one of the oldest families in the
state and had grown up from childhood in Cranston.

Of medium height, his strong lean body seemed to
sway from his small hips. He was burnt brown by
the sun and winds of the hunting field. He had a high
forehead, a straight nose with pinched nostrils. His
one blemish, the dropped shoulder, seemed only to
emphasize his other physical attributes.

Few people got beneath this crust of indifference
in Alvin's manner. He never talked of his personal
matters and sternly rebuffed any attempts at con-
fidences. Consequently, people soon ceased to inquire
what he did with the loft of the old coach house which
he had rented, in what was definitely the most undesirable part of town. To general knowledge, Nick,

the decrepit old negro who valeted Alvin, was the only other person who had ever been inside, and Nick knew too much about "gemmen's ways" to talk. All that Cranston knew was that Alvin secluded himself there when he wanted to be alone, for his own good reasons. Many a night late walkers could see a light behind the drawn curtains, but in the daytime it seemed as deserted as an old loft should be.

If Cranston had not long ago ceased to be astonished at anything Alvin might do, it would certainly have been dumbfounded at what was in the loft. For instance, if any one could have followed him one November night in 1919 when he left the Club, walked down Whelan Avenue to his retreat and entered, climbing the old stairs—if anyone had followed him that night —but, then, no one did.

Alvin was alone when he unlocked a second door at the top of the steps and walked into a room, switching on the electric light. This room had formerly been used as a cubicle where ten men slept in bunks built on the walls. There were no bunks there now. Instead, these walls were lined with book shelves that reached to the ceiling. They were loaded almost to capacity with a miscellaneous collection. The room was well lighted by electricity, and in the middle where the old coal stove used to be was a modern electric one. Near the stove was a big arm chair with a straight chair before it, obviously for the convenience of the seated one's feet. There was more furniture in the room: two other plush chairs, a big table littered with books and loose papers, and a deep-seated sofa against the wall. An expensive red and black carpet completed the general appearance of domestic comfort.

Alvin dropped into the arm chair, heaved his feet up before him and allowed himself the luxury of an oath. It was purely a luxury, for things had gone well today. Mr. Lucas, President of the Grafton Chemicals had offered him a good piece of business, and, besides, Alvin had had the pleasure of shocking several members of the Club by a statement that the world would have been better off if Germany had won the war. He liked to shock people with his ideas on politics and religion. No, he admitted, it hadn't been a bad day. And, tomorrow, he was to go hunting on Johnnie Walker. Alvin swore again with voluptuous ease.

He reached to the table and picked up a handful of papers. They were covered with pencil scribbling, his own verses. Ten years ago he had published a volume of verse under a *nom de plume,* but those critics who had not ignored it entirely had passed it by with a mere gesture. Alvin snorted when he thought of it. He pitied their taste.

He read over a few pages and laid them by with an air of injured pride—something else he never showed to the world.

For a few minutes he sat staring at the red coils of the electric stove, then, picking up a book from the table, settled down to read.

He had been reading half an hour perhaps when there came a timorous knock at the door. Slamming the book down in annoyance he called out. "You can clean up tomorrow, Nick. I told you not to bother me at night." Instead of the penitent "Yas, sar" that he expected, there came through the panels the soft, thrilling voice of a woman.

"Alvin, let me in, please."

He twisted his lithe body out of the chair in a catlike movement and opened the door. "Tommie," he said in an accent Cranston would never have recognized. It was a deep-toned accent that had a tremor in it.

The woman came in, and after he had locked the door Alvin took her by the hands and kissed her gently. "Tommie, you shouldn't have come.   I thought we agreed all this was over." There was only the softest kind of reproach in his voice.

She was dressed in a dark serge suit with a top coat over her shoulders. She slipped this off and pushed back her hair.

"Oh, Alvin, I had to. I won't stay long, but I was just around the corner and I slipped over. I came through the back way."

She had been beautiful once, and she still had that mellowed beauty which some women just under forty retain.

"He's out of town again—"

"Now, Tommie, we promised never to mention him here."

They sat down on the couch and she put her arm through his.

"You're not angry?" she said.

"Wish I were," he answered huskily. "But it can't begin all over again. You know I went to France to break it off, and now—"

"Yes, I know you did, Alvin, and you'll never know how I suffered. Promise you'll never leave again."

She put her free hand on his cheek and made him face her. He trembled at the touch and kissed her finger tips.

They sat and talked for an hour like young sweethearts in a young world. Alvin, the cynic, the snapping, growling bear of the clubroom, sat like an adoring shepherd. Alvin, the scoffer at convention, the champion of his own fancy, begged this woman he loved never to come again, while all the time his eyes begged her never to withdraw her arm from his.

Finally, the woman reminded him that it was after eleven, that she must go, and, reluctantly, he put the coat over her shoulders. Then, ever so shyly, he kissed her, and, blushing like a girl, he let her out.

Half an hour later he entered the Club, growled at the negro doorman who took his hat, and ungraciously accepted a "night-cap" from some card players who had finished their game. Then with a scowl and a vicious "Good night" he retired, warning the sleepy negro to have his boots ready at nine on peril of losing his woolly head.

V.

That Sunday in church Davis tried not to look at the back of Margie's head. Once, when the congregation rose to urge Christian soldiers on to war, she half turned and caught his eye. Davis blushed and felt very weak.

He was about two steps behind his parents coming out of church into the sunlight. Drowsy from the long internment, he did not notice that someone had stepped up beside him, until she touched his elbow and said, "Dave." -

He had never seen Margie look at him like that. It frightened him. It warmed him. His parents had walked on. There was no one within overhearing distance.

"You weren't at the party last night, Dave. We all missed you. Where've you been?"

"I've been sick," he lied.

"Sick?"

"Well, I mean busy. I'll see you some time soon."

"When? Tonight?"

"If I can get the car."

"Well you be sure; I want to talk to you."

"I'll be there," said Davis, surprised at his own assurance, "if I have to walk."

His suspension had not been a subject of conversation. Mr. Pettigrier had seemed depressed over it, and Mrs. Pettigrier had shed tears. Alvin's first words when he entered the house were, "Well, young man, what do you mean by beating up the faculty? I hear you had four men backed against the wall."

Davis stole a look at his father to see how this

frivolous attitude would be taken. To his surprise
he saw Mr. Pettigrier hide a smile behind his handkerchief.

"Chip off the old block," Alvin went on. "Only the
old man never got caught. Your education's been neglected, Davis. Don't you know that virtue consists in
never getting caught?"

Davis looked again at his father. Mrs. Pettigrier
said, "Alvin."

"Ask him," dared the jubilant guest. "Ask him
about—oh, any number of things; say, for instance,
Hallowe'en night in '98. Not so long ago."

Mr. Pettigrier clumsily changed the subject. Davis
felt warm with happiness. It was a pleasant surprise
that his father could ever have been a young rollicker.
They went in to dinner.

Alvin was full of talk. "Davis, you can hunt my
horse Thursday, if you want."

Mrs. Pettigrier intervened. "No, Alvin, he's not
having a vacation, you know. He's supposed to be
punished, not amused."

"Well, a man's got to go fox hunting, doesn't he?"

They all laughed, and, finally, it was agreed to let
him go.

In this new attitude Davis thought he understood
Margie's newly awakened interest in him. She had
probably heard what Alvin had, that he had fought off
four men at once. He began to believe it himself. No
wonder she wanted to see him tonight, he thought.
He was probably as much of a hero to her as the boys
who played yesterday.

He was apprehensive about calling on her alone. He
was used to having Tom at his elbow. He would not
dare ask Tom to take him in, and Tom would hardly
offer to, under the circumstances. But Davis was
wrong, for Tom telephoned about three o'clock and
said, "How about tonight?"

Davis invited him down to supper, and Tom came early, about six. Mr. Pettigrier must hear all about the game; he had been out of town for two days. Tom had a cut at the corner of his mouth, and he limped badly. They sat in the den and talked it over, the boys avoiding each other's eyes as boys do until they forget their latest quarrels. Mrs. Pettigrier made much of Tom's limp, and Tom pulled up his trouser leg to show the injured knee.

After supper they started in to town. Tom said, "Dave, I got something to tell you. I've been elected Captain for next year."

Davis, who was driving, reached from the steering wheel and shook hands. "That's great, Tom; honest, that's great." Both thought simultaneously of the same thing, Davis' sacrifice which made this honor possible for Tom.

"They're announcing it at the bonfire tomorrow night, and I've got to make a speech. I'm scared stiff."

Yes, thought Davis, the bonfire. They would cheer and sing the praise of the heroes, while he must stay away and neither sing nor be sung. Well, he had the satisfaction of knowing—

"You'll make the team next year, sure. I'll see you get a fair chance."

The Lucas' house had become the acknowledged gathering place for the younger citizens of the neighborhood. There is one such house in every centre of civilization, a place where youth of both genders, past the plaything age and short of the matrimonial age, convene. It is perhaps the only relic we have of the eighteenth century coffee house habit, where people dropped in, knowing, no matter what their temperaments, that they would find agreeable company.

These boys and girls who had been children together came to talk, to joke, to romp, to spoon. They were all over the first floor (Mr. and Mrs. Lucas having withdrawn above)—in the parlor, the den, the dining-room, the pantry and on the porch. You never knew who was likely to be there till you arrived. From seven-thirty to ten-thirty were the hours, for at ten-thirty Mr. Lucas came to the top of the stairs in robe and slippers and called down, "Margie!"

Unofficially, Mr. Lucas used a very modulated tone of voice, but his official capacity and the necessity of making himself heard above the din of merriment forced him to use resonant tones on Sunday nights. Sometimes, too, he had to call more than once, and this added wrath to his dignity. When Margie heard she would answer, "What, Father?" and he would reply, "Ten-thirty!"

Some of the boys used to burlesque it and imitate Mr. Lucas by simulating deep-throated, savage bellows in the half and quarter tone. They did it good-natured-ly; and Margie, although she pretended to be morti-fied, thought it very funny.

This particular Sunday night one of the more bril-liant wits had organized a mock drill so that, at the first alarm, the guests could make a quick getaway. Coats were hung over lamps and chairs, hats balanced over pictures, all in positions for a quick donning.

"Now when I give the alarm, jump into your things and see how quickly we can empty the house." The master of ceremonies stood in the hall, watch in hand and bellowed, "Margie!"

Boys and girls, all except Margie, who alternated between pouting and fuming, pushed their arms into their garments, shook the pictures so that their hats fell on their heads and scurried out the front door.

"Not bad," admitted the timekeeper. "Once more."

They did it again and again, each time trying to do something more outrageously absurd than before. They leaped out of windows, pretended to rescue each other and laughed and yelled at each new prank until Mr.

and Mrs. Lucas upstairs feared for their homestead.

Finally, flushed and still buoyant, they ceased and hung their garments in preparation for the genuine alarm which would come in half an hour.

Now for the first time Davis had a chance to speak to Margie.

"I'm glad you came, Dave," she said. "Come out here; I want to tell you something."

Wondering and fluttering Davis followed her out on the porch and sat down in the hammock beside her. The chill night air made him shiver, but he would have shivered anyhow. It was dark and quiet there, and he was alone with her. Davis held his breath.

"I think you're marvelous, Dave. Tom told me all about it, how you took all the blame so he could play."

Davis was looking out into the garden, but he knew her eyes were on him. He dared not face her, yet he knew he was expected to do or say something. "Oh, well—" he said and stopped.

"If I were a boy I'd be much prouder of that than of winning a letter."

"I don't know," he said. "I didn't have much choice." Davis thought the tone of his voice was unusual. Hers was different, too. Soft and more personal than he had ever heard it. Emboldened, he looked at her. She was leaning toward him earnestly, with interest, he thought. Their eyes met. He forgot he was cold outside, because of the burning flame within.

They talked of various subjects now—parties, movies, Dr. Peckam's sermon. Time passed unnoticed. They both shivered and chattered with cold, but did not deign to notice. Then, suddenly, Margie said, "Oh, what time is it?"

They went indoors, and every one was gone. The clock in the hall was a quarter to eleven.

"Is that you, Margie?" Mr. Lucas' official voice bounded down the steps.

"Yes, Father, I was out on the porch. I didn't hear you."

"Whom are you with?"

Davis slunk into his overcoat. Margie answered, "He's going now."

"I asked you *who*," came from the firmament above.

"It's me, sir," put in Davis weakly. "Good night, sir. Good night, Margie." This last greeting was in an undertone as he slipped out the door, just too late to miss hearing the exasperated bellow, "Who's *me?*"

Tom was sitting behind the wheel with the motor running. "Uh-huh, young man, sneaking in a little extra time. Looks pretty bad to me."

But Davis was too happy to mind jibes now. He was still shivering. He slouched down in the seat and hunched his shoulders. And in his mind he was running over and over the gramophone record which sang:

"Margie, you are my inspiration, Margie."

VI

Mr. Jackson Pettigrier sat in the smoking car of the New York Express, waiting for the porter to make up his berth. He felt the train gather itself together like a great serpent and move off. He saw the Cranston station slip back into the darkness.

He was strangely apprehensive that night, and he knew that Davis' trouble at school made him so. He told himself repeatedly it was a trivial thing but found logic, as always, a poor comforter. He was not less apprehensive as he rationalized. His experience with life had not been one to foster optimism.

Jackson Pettigrier's father's father had been a landed gentleman of the South. In '61 he had gone off to the war with his son, the one to ride behind Jeb Stuart, the other to follow Stonewall Jackson. The elder had never returned, and the younger came back to a home of shattered windows and weedy gardens. In time he mended the windows, weeded the gardens and married one whose only bounty was a name as ancient and honorable as his own. Together they lived in the patched-up house, wearing clothes their parents had cast off, using silverware of more prosperous days. Nobody knew how they lived, how they kept their defiant dignity and old-fashioned grace, or, strangest of all, how they managed to send their son, Jackson, to college. But they did.

Within the year in which Jackson Pettigrier graduated, both his parents died, leaving the home mortgaged to the gables and years-old creditors waiting in the hall. Somewhere Jackson had learned that debts were to be paid. He sold the place to strangers, the portraits and silver to better-to-do branches of the family. He said goodbye to his neighbors and went to Cranston to make a living.

He had gone there with the idea of winning a scholarship and of studying medicine at the State University, but an intervening circumstance caused him to give up this idea and to take a position in a bank. That circumstance was his meeting with Molly Davis. For three years he worked, worked with a concentrated energy that won him promotion over several elder heads. He married Molly Davis and built a home in the country.

There were three children and ten happy years. Each year found him working harder and rejoicing in the opportunity and incentive. He was offered the vice-presidency of the Dial Engineering Company. It meant more money with the added burden of being away from home a great deal. He accepted it because he wished that nothing should be left undone for his young family. Cranston began to call him a well-to-do man.

Then had come the time when half of this family was taken away. Jackson Pettigrier thought of it as he gazed out the blind window. Since that day he had felt how completely men were at the mercy of Fate. He had come to know that it was not earnestness, ambition or virtue that made men's lives, but only uncontrollable circumstance. An ever-present ghost of futility had haunted him since that day. He wondered if human effort were at all worth while and whether a relenting Fate would give him another chance to be happy.

He had continued to work. If anything, he worked harder than ever. Dr. Peckam had come to him after the tragedy and reminded him that God had mercifully left him one child. On that one child fell all the love and devotion that had once been divided among three.

Now the child was growing up. In another year or so, thought the father, he would go to college. Mr. Pettigrier was determined that Davis should have everything to make those years there the happiest and fullest of his life—just as they had been in his own life. Davis should, of course, be elected to the Owl Club, to which Louis Davis, Alvin Martin and himself had belonged. He must have the means to go with the best crowd and to do what he wanted. Nothing was too good for a Pettigrier, and Davis was the last of that name.

But these were only the advantages Davis was to have. Above all, he was to graduate with honors and take his place in the world. If Mr. Pettigrier had one ruling passion it was that Davis should make a name for himself in some profession, preferably in medicine. There were enough blue-blooded good-for-nothings, thought the father. His son must take his place in the vanguard of success. Deep in his heart was an aversion to business. Jackson Pettigrier knew too much about the drudgery of it. "He'll never need money," murmured a man looking out of a train window. "I've seen to that. I only hope Molly and I will live to see another Pettigrier whom people will call a leader."

The porter put his head in to say that the berth was ready. Mr. Pettigrier nodded but remained where he was. The trouble at school worried him. He hoped Davis wasn't going to turn out one of those black sheep that good families breed so often. The more he thought of it, the more he realized what a factor the boy was in his own life. His happiness or sorrow rested almost entirely on those narrow, irresponsible shoulders. Let Davis turn out a failure or a scoundrel, and all these years of concentrated, grinding labor had been in vain.

He fumbled with the newspaper that lay across his

knees. How he hated traveling! Some day, perhaps, after Davis had been established in a profession, Jackson Pettigrier would retire and live as a southern gentleman should, at home with his wife and friends.

VII

The Monday morning after his thrilling talk with Margie, Davis slept late. There was no school for him that week, and as his father had gone to New York, he was not called. It was half-past nine when he looked at his wrist watch. Vaguely he wondered what would be his status during this week of banishment. Would he be confined to the house or punished in any way? He knew he must devote a good portion ·of the time to his studies, so as not to lose valuable ground. Perhaps his father had left orders below.

With infinite leisure he arose and dressed. A place was still set for him at the table. Manuel brought in hot eggs and toast, volunteering that "the Madam" had not been down. The maid had said she was still asleep.

Davis took his books into the den and turned over a few pages. His mind wandered. Why, he was thinking, not make hay while the sun shone? Why not see a lot of Margie this week? Why not go and see her this afternoon? The question was, would his mother allow him to go? He might beg the question by going before Mrs. Pettigrier awoke, but he knew that Margie went to Miss Fontaine's School until lunch time. She had told him so last night. He wondered if she had meant anything by it.

Abandoning all pretense of work, he pushed the books aside. Mrs. Pettigrier might awake any minute and send for him. He thought of Alvin. He would take his books, go to Alvin's office, sit in a corner and study till the hour came. He would have to face an interview that night, he thought, but, as Dr. Peckam had said only yesterday, there is a pearl of great price in every man's life.

Davis picked up three books at random and hurried to the garage. Three-quarters of an hour later he walked into Alvin's office. The secretary showed him into the private room where Alvin was wont to growl at his clients across the desk.

The man of law seemed unnecessarily disturbed by the unexpected visitor.

"What's wrong?" he snapped.

Davis, wondering mildly at the assumption, said, "Not a thing. I only want to sit somewhere and study till about two o'clock. I've got an engagement in town."

Alvin's manner softened, and he pointed to a big leather chair by the window. "Help yourself. All I ask is that you keep still. We'll go to lunch at one."

He did his best to keep still, but his mind refused to cope with history, Latin and French, which he tried in succession. Every time he moved the leather chair squeaked, but Alvin, rattling away at a stack of papers, seemed not to notice.

At twelve-thirty the telephone rang, and Alvin said, "Yes, Molly. I don't know. Yes, he's here now, working hard. We're going to lunch together."

They went to the City Club. The boy was bashful among so many older men. He noticed how lively the servants moved when his host spoke to them. He was getting nervous over his intended visit. He hoped Mr. Lucas would be out.

Luncheon over, he thanked Alvin and drove to the Lucases. It occurred to him that it might be too early, that they might be still at table. He drove around the block for fifteen minutes. Finally, summoning all his courage, he went up boldly and rang the bell. The stern-faced English butler opened the door, but before Davis could ask for Margie, she appeared, herself, and welcomed him with feigned surprise. He was certain from her smile that she expected him.

They went to a moving picture show. Davis sat in the dark beside her, scarcely daring to breathe for fear of breaking the magic spell of her presence.

"What did your family say about your suspension?" Margie wanted to know, as they drove back to her house.

"Not much—yet."

"I should think they'd be proud of what you did. Do they know the whole story?"

"No. I don't want to tell them about Tom and the others."

Margie's admiration expanded. She told Davis he was wonderful.

"Oh, I don't know. Most any one would have done it."

"No, they wouldn't," Margie insisted. "Very few would."

Davis failed to continue the conversation. His joy was complete. Margie admired him, liked him; soon, perhaps, she might love him. He blessed the day that he was dismissed from the football squad.

Had he known Margie's sex better he would never have jumped at such conclusions. Experience had not taught him the secrets of the feminine fancy. It never entered his head that lack of competition had anything to do with his sudden prosperity. Nor did it occur to him that women's words are seldom to be taken at face value. He might have remembered, had he cared to, that Margie, during the afternoon, had applied the adjective "wonderful" to the pictures, to Saturday's game and to Sunday's sermon as well as to his own actions. She had not told him that she loved him, yet she confessed that none too tender passion for the hero of the picture, for a box of chocolates Davis bought her, and for his dilapidated car.

No doubts or besetting fears disturbed Davis Pettigrier as he told his love good-night and promised—
at her instigation—to call again tomorrow. He went
off in a sad state of intoxication, an inebriation far
worse, both as regards present state and after-effects,
than that caused by alcohol. As he drove along he
swore an oath to heaven that he would henceforth
live a life of nobility, self-sacrifice and altruism for
the sake and by the grace of Margie Lucas.

"Davis," said his mother when he closed the front
door behind him, "I don't know what's getting into
you. I used to be able to rely on you, but now you
have to be watched every minute. Don't you know
you're being punished for your disgraceful conduct
at school? I should think you'd be so ashamed of
causing your father and me all that humiliation that
you'd try to make up for it. Instead of that you run
off and spend the day in some mysterious manner when
you should be studying. Now where have you been?"

"I had lunch with Alvin and then—well, I went to
the movies."

"To the movies! Heavens above. You get dismissed—"

"Only suspended, Mother."

"Don't interrupt me. Get dismissed from school and
spend your time at the movies. I don't know what
your father will say. Now after dinner you take your
books to the den and try to do some serious work. I'm
going to town, and when I get back I want you to show
me what you've done. No, I may be late. I'll see it in
the morning."

Mrs. Pettigrier had a hobby for slum work. Once
or twice a week, always during her husband's absence,
she had the chauffeur set her down in the Italian quarter of town, and return for her three or four hours
later. She always said that when her husband was
away she was so lonely she had to do something to

keep her mind busy. Calling on these poor families and seeing after their needs in a small way helped her in her own troubles. She did not care much for organized work of this sort, for, as she told Dr. Peckam, what these poor folk needed was the personal touch.

By dint of an unprecedented display of energy, Davis accomplished enough work that night and the next morning to be permitted to keep his appointment that afternoon. And so the week sped by, the happiest of his life, thought the boy, and wished he had drawn a longer suspension. He saw and thought so much of Margie that he completely forgot to hunt Alvin's horse on Thursday and looked forward with apprehension to the ragging he would get for it Sunday.

That Sunday Dr. Peckam came to dinner. The Pettigriers waited for him after church and brought him out. As Mrs. Pettigrier entered her front door followed by the guest, her husband and son, she saw Alvin lying full length on the living-room sofa, reading the morning paper. She had utterly forgotten about his being there. But it was too late now, and Alvin's first words justified her misgivings. He had not looked up when he heard the door open, but as they entered the hall he called out. "Well, what did he teach you today? How to be good in three lessons."

Mrs. Pettigrier moaned softly, and the man of God cleared his throat. Alvin jumped up and said almost graciously, "I beg your pardon, Dr. Peckam, but we old heathens, you know how we are."

"Yes, yes," sighed the Doctor, "I know. How are you, sir?"

So that crisis was past, thought the disturbed lady. She wished she could get a word with Alvin alone before they went to dinner. She looked at him appealingly as he helped her off with her coat.

"Yes, Alvin, as a matter of fact you were right," Mr. Pettigrier remarked with forced ease. "Dr.

Peckam did tell us how to be good this morning. A real bang-up sermon on 'Consider the lilies of the field.'"

"What about them?" asked Alvin, pretending not to notice his hostess' entreating frown.

"They toil not, neither do they spin," put in Davis triumphantly.

"Good for you, fox-hunter, and what *do* they do to be worth considering—go to church?"

"Alvin—please," said Mrs. Pettigrier.

"I'm sorry, again. Doctor, please forgive my curiosity. I just want to know, is that a Biblical text? It sounds so much like good pagan poetry."

"Ah, Mr. Martin, I see you don't understand the spirit of Christianity. That's why you misinterpret holy parables."

"Well, maybe you're right. I mean, of course you're right. I don't understand Christianity at all. I wish you would help me to, sometime. What's that about more joy in heaven over one sinner who repenteth? Just think what a fine time they'd have up there if you converted me."

He said it so seriously that no one was sure how to take it. Before it was necessary to answer, dinner was announced.

Mrs. Pettigrier plucked Alvin's arm as they went in. Their eyes met. She pleaded silently with him, and he looked back a penitent half-promise.

During dinner Alvin turned his attention on Davis and advised him in his father's hearing not to go back to school at all. "How're you going to court that girl and study, too? If you forget your hunting engagements, you'll never remember your alphabet."

Only once at table was Mrs. Pettigrier alarmed. That was when Dr. Peckam was telling with righteous warmth how he had refused to marry in his church a woman of unenviable notoriety.

"Perfectly right, Dr .Peckam," she said.

"Perfectly," rejoined Alvin, wagging his finger at Davis. "It doesn't do to say to sinners nowadays, 'Go and sin no more.' The time is past when you could forgive your brother seventy times seven."

After dinner Mrs. Pettigrier left the men together in the living-room enjoying their coffee. Curiosity made Dr. Peckam reckless. "How is it, Mr. Martin, that you, who profess agnosticism, know the Bible so well?"

Alvin roused himself from his own meditation like a surly dog it were best to let lie.

"Well, Doctor, I read almost anything. I'm very fond of biography and history. Jesus Christ is a very interesting character to me. Even more so than Napoleon."

"We seem to agree on that point, but we differ in that you don't admire Christ."

"Oh, yes, I do," corrected Alvin. "I not only admire him, but I agree with him."

"Then why don't you come and worship Him?"

Alvin picked up the morning paper. "The weather man said fair and warm today. Is he right?"

"Yes," admitted the minister warily.

"Well, then, you agree with him. Why don't you worship him?"

Davis looked askance at Alvin. Jokes were all right, but this was going too far, he thought, calling Christ a weather man. Mr. Pettigrier shook his head and glanced at Dr. Peckam, waiting for him to denounce the infidel.

"My dear Mr. Martin, really I don't know that I should argue with you, sir. You have no sense of reverence. I feel that the best thing I can do is to pray for you."

"Alvin," said Mr. Pettigrier, "what you should do

is to make yourself go to church. Give God a chance
to come into your life and open your eyes."

"Now, Jackson, tell me how many times have you
heard of Christ going to church? You don't know?
As far as I remember—once, and that time he picked
up a whip and chased out a lot of business men. I
never heard of him chasing any in, and that's what you-
all are trying to do, both of you."

"You have a clever tongue, Mr. Martin, but no religion at all in your make-up. You twist everything
around to suit your own fancy."

"I must beg to differ with you again, sir. I have
plenty of religion, but no theology, and I can't for
the life of me understand how you ministers ever did
the twisting you have done. I told you I agreed with
Christ. I'll tell you why more precisely. When
people were hungry, he fed them; when they were
lame, halt and blind, he cured them. But has that anything to do with putting on robes and going through
ritual? Don't you know that the ritual you go through
is the essence of paganism? I can't see how you twisted
Christ's simple teachings into what you have. Another
thing—one day I went through all the prayers in the
church service; and do you know, sentence for sentence,
what was the proportion of selfishness? I mean
prayers for one's own health and prosperity?"

"I don't care to hear your figures, Mr. Martin. I
can only say I'm surprised that a man of your intelli-
gence shouldn't read deeper into things than you have.
You don't seem to realize Christ is God Himself in
the flesh."

"How could he be his own father and his own son?
Dr. Peckam, what I don't understand is why your
profession is determined to make it so difficult. Why
not take it in its obvious way that Christ was Mary's
son, that he was a great leader of thought, that he
was far ahead of the times (and still is), that he was

an idealist who became a menace to the government
and was executed. There have been plenty of such
cases, yet we don't build pagan temples to the poor
wretches."

"Mr. Martin, I cannot argue with a man who in-
sinuates that our Lord was—was of tainted birth. I
can only tell you, not argue, mind you, tell you that
He came primarily to minister unto the souls of men,
not their bodies. Now don't interrupt me, sir, with
one of your quotations trimmed down for the occasion."

"No quotation this time, Dr. Peckam, I promise. I
only want to tell you a story about souls. I was in a
French hospital, and there was a man who had died.
They had put the screen in front of his bed as they
always do, and I suppose he had lain there for half
an hour when an officer rushed in all excited. It seems
that the deceased had had information in his head that
they wanted. Well, they got after that poor body.
They used serums and gases and things I knew nothing
of for two hours, and then I heard the dead man ask
for a drink of water. The officer asked him some questions which he answered. He breathed and groaned
for two days and then died again. I always wondered,
Doctor, where was the immortal soul for that half hour
the body was dead."

"The only solution is that he wasn't dead. The
doctors might have been wrong." This was Mr. Pettigrier's contribution.

"The ways of the Lord are inscrutable," said the
clergyman.

"I agree with you there," said Alvin.

For a few minutes no one spoke. Through it all,
Davis had sat mute. He felt keenly capable of understanding it all. Instinctively he felt that Alvin was
wrong, although he could not see around his arguments.

Dr. Peckam used the few moments of silence to

think of some way to answer this enemy of the faith. Finally, he spoke.

"Your anecdote only serves to prove, if indeed proof is necessary, that the soul is immortal, that those who believe in Christ live forever."

"Fearful thought, isn't it, Doctor? Live forever! As if any one could want to." He seemed almost musing to himself. "I know when I've had enough."

"Ah, Mr. Martin, not live in this vale of tears and woes, but in another world, a world of—"

"Not milk and honey, I hope. Tell me, Doctor, and I mean this in all seriousness, do you honestly believe that a reasonable God would give men reason, and then condemn them for believing in what their reason taught them?"

"But, my dear sir, that is why Christ came, to teach men things beyond the power of their own reason. To answer your question: Yes, sir, I honestly believe God will condemn men of the Christian era who deny the teachings of the holy Church."

"And, Dr. Peckam, which Church is the holy Church? And what of the many centuries of men before the Christian era, and the millions that follow Mohammed, Buddha and Confucius?   Are they doomed to damnation? Have you studied the teaching of these men? Well, I have; and essentially they are not much different from Christ's."

"Mr. Martin," the clergyman spoke slowly and with decision, "you are too clever, too mentally acrobatic for a man of my years and ability. I am only sorry that so good a cause as mine should have so mean a defender. I can only tell you that I *do* believe everything I profess to believe. I believe the world needs religion, more than reason or food or any material matter. If I didn't think so, I wouldn't give my life and efforts, such as they are, to it. When you have seen as much of life as I have, perhaps you'll understand, perhaps not. I can't rebut your arguments, but they do not shake my faith. I believe in Jesus Christ's promises, though I have only a gentleman's word for them. 'Lo, I am with you always, even unto the end of the world.' "

The little man looked so pitifully defiant, so like a tired fox turning hopelessly to face the outnumbering pack, that Alvin felt rather ashamed of himself.

Mrs. Pettigrier had entered inconspicuously during the last speech. She went up to the little minister and laid her hand on his, that was wrinkled and shaky.

"So do we all, Dr. Peckam. You mustn't mind Alvin. I'm sorry he's been so disagreeable. I should have thought him more of a gentleman than to behave as he has."

Alvin turned crimson. She did not look at him, nor did her husband. Davis stole a hidden glance to see the effect of this stab. He knew, as did his father, that nothing could hurt more than these words. Secretly they both thought them too sharp.

"I must be going," said Alvin in a changed voice. No man would have dared insult him as this woman had. Bowing coldly he started to leave the room, but Dr. Peckam rose, too, and stopped him.

"No, please, Mr. Martin, please don't go off like that. Mrs. Pettigrier, I'm sure, has put it too strongly. Certainly you have as much right to your opinion as I to mine. My doctrine would be of little value if it could not stand opposition."

Mr. Pettigrier added his persuasion, and, together, they all but forced Alvin back into his chair. Mrs. Pettigrier said nothing and avoided meeting anyone's eyes. Alvin sat down and looked coldly at the grate. The tide of battle had completely changed, it seemed to Davis. He had never seen Alvin humbled before. It all seemed to vindicate his own faith.

"Perhaps, if you're going in town soon, you could
drop me by the rectory, Mr. Martin."

"Delighted, sir."   Alvin was frigid politeness.

The two guests remained half an hour longer and
went off together. When the door closed behind them,
Jackson Pettigrier turned to his wife.

"Molly, you've hurt his feelings terribly. You must
make up with him somehow."

To his surprise, she burst into passionate tears and
flung herself upon him crying. "Oh, I'll never make
it up. I hate him, hate him! Jackson, please don't
go away this week. Oh, please don't!"

Davis slipped into the study, wiping his eyes with
the knuckles of his two hands.

VIII

It is an interesting question, and one not without its philosophical value, whether the times we enjoy go fastest or whether we enjoy certain times because they do go fastest—interesting, perhaps, but immaterial to the students of Barclay School. Came the Christmas holiday and whirred across their horizon like a wild duck on Chesapeake Bay. It no sooner came than it was gone.

In that impatient period Davis experienced a relative happiness. Freed from the fetters of discipline and duty, life seemed once more a thing of joy.

Hunting the fox was his keenest pleasure. It thrilled him to see the hounds clustered behind Huntsman Mike Riley, jogging to the meet, to see the Master roll up in his big car and mount resplendent in his scarlet coat. But these were only *hors d'oeuvres* for the feast that followed. There was the "tut-tu, tut-tu" of the horn, the crash of the hounds in full cry, the dark, stiff fences as seen between a horse's ears. Here Davis glutted his love of old romance and adventure. There was that fearless knight, Sir Alvin Martin, whose reputation it was never to turn his horse's head from anything. Davis worshipped the Alvin of the hunting field—and envied him, too. He copied Alvin's slouching post as they trotted from covert to covert and his jockey-seat as they galloped over fields. Sometimes Davis tried to follow him, but too often, when Alvin, in sheer bravado, picked the biggest panel to jump, Davis looked for a gap. There were times when he would make himself do what he was afraid to do, and then he would rejoice and think of his great-grandfather who rode behind Jeb Stuart and of his grandfather who marched behind Stonewall Jackson. Some day, Davis vowed, he would ride steeplechases as Alvin did. The only thing he preferred to fox-hunting was watching the point-to-point races in the spring.

When it was very cold the ponds would freeze, and there would be hockey. Davis was usually the poorest player on the ice, but none played with a more gallant disregard of personal injury. His skinned elbows, and swollen knees were cherished badges of honor fairly won. Davis considered it a good day if he could skate all morning and hunt all afternoon.

He was consciously happy during the days, but in the evenings when he went to the holiday parties this pleasure was of a subtler sort. He tortured himself exquisitely in the age-old method of romantic lovers, with the thought of his own unworthiness. He considered his passion too sacred for the world's recognition and kept it, in fact, so secret that even its object scarcely conceived it.

Behind the Christmas vacation came the Winter Term. It sat upon the lap of time:

> "As idle as a painted ship
> Upon a painted ocean."

New Year resolutions went the way of all good intentions. Barclay School rode in the trough of indolence and boredom until, as it seemed, without warning, wind filled the sails of time, and existence began to move, for the Spring Holidays had come.

There was crêpe on the cross in Trinity Church this time of year that people called Lent, but Nature refused to be sombre, and so did her children. Baseball and sunshine. Baseball and showers. Wet pavements, wet grass. The shop girls giggled as they waited for the trolleys. The farmers' daughters leaned from the kitchen windows and shouted at the men in the fields.

With spring came the point-to-point races, and Davis went to them all. He saw Alvin rise out of the dirt, spitting blood one Saturday and saw him win in a driving finish the next.

More showers, more sunshine and then time stopped like a bawky horse. The spring term began, and beyond this burning desert one could see a green garden with fountains and fruit—or was it only a mirage, thought the boys of Barclay School.

IX

In the autumn of 1921 Davis Pettigrier and his three friends went to Kingston University. Phil Parsons, true to his form, took the step upward with ease, but Tom Stevenson, Joe Watson and Davis were successful only, quoting Phil, "by the grace of God and a fast outfield." However that may have been, when they signed their names one after another in the big registration book they were equal in the sight of dean and man.

It was fully two weeks before they began to realize that they were only some three hundred miles north of Barclay School, and not actually on a different planet. Those two weeks had been a tiresome round of speakers telling them they were no longer boys but men, moreover that they were Kingston men; that Kingston men were the pick of the country; that each and every one of them was keeping out fifteen other applicants; of tradesmen who wanted their patronage; of upperclassmen who wanted to sign them up for debating halls and social service work; of sophomores who made them do idiotic hazing freaks; of a feeling of importance dwindling into one of insignificance.

And now the newness of it was beginning to harden into the commonplace. The little black skull cap that freshmen had to wear changed its earnest snugness over the brows for a clinging sort of nonchalance on the back of the head. They ceased to pay attention to the notices in the *Campus* requiring the presence of the class of 1925 to an address by famous doctors, preachers or officials; they began to ignore the sophomores who scowled at them as they passed each other on the walks; and, most significant of all, they no longer sprinted to their lectures for fear of being late.

The last two years had wrought little change in Davis Pettigrier. He had still the long, frail body, the spindle legs, the pale plain-girlish face, the grey eyes that looked so unexpectedly virile. Time had stretched the frail body making it still thinner, and deposited a patch of almost invisible bristles on the narrow chin; but that was all.

During the first term at Kingston, Davis met so many people that faces and names ran together and were blurred. He who had held a high opinion of mankind was mildly disillusioned at the low standard of what the speakers had proclaimed to be the pick of the country. He had expected all of them to be charming and gentlemanly, but as a matter of fact for the most part they were boring and often coarse in conversation and manner. Davis explained it to himself and to Tom by the fact that the great majority were "Yankees." Being southerners themselves they found this explanation acceptable.

Another shock he received was at the shameless manner in which many of the undergraduates got credit for work that was not their own. The senior who lived above them boasted that he had not written an essay for three years. He had collected the best efforts of the class just ahead of him and handed them in as his own. Another scoffed at the idea of attending compulsory chapel.

"All you have to do is to get someone to bring you a card, sign it and slip it in the box Monday morning."

As for chastity and temperance, these qualities seemed conspicuous by their absence.

In fact it seemed to Davis before he was half-way through the term that the undergraduate body was divided into two classes; those who were attractive and dissolute, and those who were unattractive and

virtuous. For example there was the insignificant looking sophomore, Damp, across the hall who was the
soul of virtue and propriety. Damp was hollow-
chested, pimple-faced and he stammered. When he
did manage to convey a thought it was of the most
vapid insipidity.

"Poor Damp," Davis said, "I feel sorry for him.
He tries so hard and he means well."

"I wouldn't waste much pity on him," replied Tom,
Davis' roommate. "Nature protects fools like that
from knowing how impossible they are. That's what
Phil said about people who look like they need pity."

"Well, I hope so. We ought to be pretty decent to
him, I think. Let's drop in and talk to him sometime,
Tom."

"No, thanks," Tom answered; and then after a
thoughtful pause went on. "Look here, Dave, next
year we'll be up for club elections and now's the time
to make the right kind of friends. Instead of feeling
sorry for Damp, you ought to take the trouble to meet
some of the people that will do you some good. You're
too independent, and those who don't know you don't
understand.

Davis looked up quickly. "You mean I ought to
boot-lick around some of these club men, do you?
Not me. When I find out whom I like I'll stick with
them, but I won't do any more."

"No one said anything about boot-licking, but there's
a certain amount of diplomacy necessary in college.
You ask anyone. For instance, you oughtn't to look
so shocked every time those fellows upstairs say something you don't approve of. They're both in the Owl
Club, and if they get to think we're a pair of blue-
noses we'll never get anywhere."

"If that's the way to get along in college I don't
care much for it."

"It's all right to talk big now, Dave, but next year

it'll be different. You certainly want to go to your father's and uncle's club, don't you? I know your father wants you to."

Davis said no more, but he noticed as time went on that Tom was not quite the same as he was at school. He used new expressions he had picked up lately and they sounded strangely from his tongue. He seemed to become quickly intimate with strangers, calling them by their nick-names and playing bridge in their rooms. Sometimes he brought them to his own room and acted very unlike himself, especially in the way he smoked and swore. Twice in such company Davis noticed him cut Damp pointedly.

One night when Davis was working late, Tom came in with a strange glint in his eye and Davis was almost sure he had been drinking. After that Tom took to going to the city with a crowd of swaggering dandies. Davis had a feeling that Tom was a little ashamed of him. They began to see less of each other, and Davis began to take on an air of defiant melancholy from being alone so much. He started going to see Phil and Joe, but before long discovered that they also were forming a new set of friends.

One day late in November Tom reopened the subject.

"Dave, how about coming to the city with a few of us tonight? We'll stir up some fun and you'll enjoy it."

"Who's going?"

"Bob Johnson and a few others. Mighty nice fellows, you ought to know them. Snap out of it, Dave, this is college, not a nursery, you know."

"What do you do up there? Go to night clubs and drink liquor?"

"Yes, a little of each. Why don't you come?"

"Because I don't know the fellows and don't think I want to."

"It's mighty polite of you to speak about my friends that way."

"Well, maybe they think and speak the same way of me."

Tom laughed affectionately, and his voice softened. "I'm only telling you for your own good that this is the crowd you ought to go round with. If you don't care about enjoying yourself up here, I suppose it's none of my business."

Davis thought it all over after Tom had gone. There was something in what Tom had said, he admitted. After all, there was not much sense in making a recluse of himself. He wanted to have friends but the idea of campaigning for them was distasteful, especially among those whom Tom had picked out. They were a swaggering, ultra-sophisticated lot, with all the qualities of their type that he disliked. They fancied themselves young men about town and talked with practised ease about the price of gin and the reputation of women.

Still, argued Davis, if Tom liked them they must have some attraction. Phil and Joe, too, knew and liked many of the same group. He decided he would make an effort to know them better.

He did make a modest, half-hearted effort, but with little success. He was actually unable to make himself congenial. He could not get over some ideas of decency and decorum that had been drilled into him at home and although he did not utter his disapproval he showed it very plainly by his blushes and embarrassed attempts at conversation. He was perfectly willing to give up and retire into his shell when the Christmas holidays came.

Back in Cranston he found contentment. He had not realized until he returned how much he missed home. There was his father consumed with pride at having a son in college. Mr. Pettigrier listened greedily to all the anecdotes of the freshman's first term, and supplemented them with tales of his own. His mother, too, made much of him, saying that she knew he had found his home training a great help in overcoming temptations he had met or would soon meet. Alvin chaffed him, asking whether he had been drunk yet and how many times he had been up before the dean.

Margie Lucas also returned from her finishing school. When Davis called on her (which he did boldly and alone at the first opportunity) he found her radiant with welcome. Davis thought he had never seen her so charming or so glad to see him. New and wonderful hopes filled his breast. He forgot his diffidence; and appeared at his best for almost the first time in her presence.

They sat often on the porch in the hammock where she had first kindled his hopes, and chattered like a pair of unspoiled children.

Davis took Margie to many parties that vacation. Mrs. Lucas said that Davis was one of the few with whom she "trusted" Margie. When Alvin heard this he said that he did not consider it a compliment to be called "safe," but Davis did. He was glad somebody appreciated his good qualities.

But all good things, unlike all evil ones, have their endings. Christmas passed, the New Year came, and vacation was drawing to a close. The last night at home there was a dance in town. Tom had telephoned Davis the day before and asked him if he were taking Margie.

Davis said, "I was just going to ask her."

"So was I. What do you say we toss a coin for the privilege?"

Davis agreed and called for heads. Tom on his end of the line examined the coin, and said ruefully, "You win." Davis was almost sorry. Tom was such a sport to give him the chance. Yes, there was no doubt of it, Tom was the best fellow in the world and Margie the best girl.

He called for her that evening, and stood hat in hand waiting for her to come down stairs. When she did come, it was in a black evening dress that reached to her ankles. Her proud head with the tilted chin and tiny pug nose, her white arms and gleaming shoulders, her rounded body filling out to perfection the old-fashioned dress—all of her, even the lace-fringed fan in her left hand, fairly took his breath away. She looked a queen stepping out of an old romance. A line of poetry, he knew not whose, ran through his brain:

"Earth has not anything to show more fair."

"Good evening," she said, archly conscious of the impression she had made.

Davis was on the point of saying, "Margie, you're the most beautiful thing in the world," but found it completely beyond his power. Instead, he said: "That's a right good looking dress you have on, Margie."

She smiled sweetly, and picking up her cape from a chair handed it to him. He put it tenderly over her shoulders. Was it his imagination, or did she really linger a golden moment in his arms? She went into the living-room and kissed her father and mother goodbye.

"Now, behave yourself, Margie, and come home early," Davis heard Mrs. Lucas say; and with a rustling of a newspaper he heard Mr. Lucas add his approval.

When she came out into the hall, she took his arm of her own accord. As they went down the front steps she swayed gently against him and to his embarrassment Davis felt against his elbow the gentle pressure of her breast. Instinctively he pulled away, ashamed of his vulgarity in having to admit the existence of her body.

He helped her into the car. She sat close to him while he drove, and at every corner he felt her shoulder brush against his, and the fur of her collar against his cheek.

"Tomorrow," she said, "you go away and I won't see you till Easter."

" Yes," said he, "till Easter."

"I get awfully homesick at school. Do you?"

"Well, maybe not homesick, but I miss people—at home."

"So do I. You'll write to me, won't you, Dave?"

"You know I will, Margie." It was the closest he had ever come to making love to her, and she replied encouragingly:

"I don't know so, I only hope so."

He started her off at the dance. Like an airy something she seemed, moving with the lightness of shadows. Her lips were a few inches from his cheek, and he could feel rather than hear her voice as she spoke. The orchestra played a new tune, called "I'm Just Wild About Harry," and Davis was substituting another name, when someone tapped him on the shoulder and claimed his partner.

He wandered about for an hour, cutting in generously on Margie, and bravely doing his "duty-dances." He ran into Tom who was carrying on a dull conversation with a stoutly-built florid young man whom Davis did not know. When Tom saw Davis he broke off the conversation, mumbled an introduction and turned his interest on him.

"You won the toss-up, Dave, but I claim compensation. I'm going to sit out this next one with her."

"Sure. Help yourself."

The stout young man butted in and offered them a drink, which they both declined. By his hard accent, Davis knew him to be an out-of-towner, but he had missed the name. Soon the three of them drifted apart.

Tom stayed out with Margie for two dances. When they came in, Davis noticed their faces were flushed and concluded they had taken a drive. He cut in; but before he had gone many steps, was himself superseded. He noticed that it was by the stout young man Tom had introduced.

Walking back to the stag line someone punched him in the ribs and said, "Cheer up. The worst is yet to come." It was Phil Parsons.

"Say, Phil, who's that dancing with Margie?"

Phil did not know. They went outside to have a smoke. Later on, Davis found Tom and asked him about the stranger.

"Oh, that? His name's Schnell, all the way from Cincinnati. He's working here for a year to learn the fertilizer business, then he's going back. He's a millionaire come out of the west."

"Good fellow, too," put in Joe Watson who, seeing them together, had joined them. "He gave me a drink."

Joe looked as if someone had given him several. Davis shook his head when he thought what a difference one term at college had made in his friends.

The orchestra started the Blue Danube Waltz, and Davis and Tom both headed toward the floor with a single intention. "Toss you for it," said Davis. He flipped a coin and won.

"Who's this cowboy friend of yours?" he chided Margie as they waltzed.

"Roswell Schnell. He's not bad. Sort of dumb, that's all. He means well."

"Up at college," said Davis with superiority, "that's the worst thing you can say about a man, except maybe 'He can't help it.' Can't Schnell help it either?"

"Hush," she said, squeezing his hand. The next moment Schnell cut in, and Davis went scowling to the wall.

The party lasted till two o'clock, and then with smothered yawns and tired limbs Margie and Davis drove home. She was even more lovely in her weariness, he thought, stealing a glance at the languid little figure beside him. They had not much to say till he stopped at her house and followed her up the steps to the front door. He took her key and opened it. She held the knob in her left hand behind her and offered her right.

"Good-bye, old man, and good luck."

"Old man." She had never called him that before. It was the way she might have spoken to a brother, or a dear friend, or even to a lover. He took her hand and she let it lie between his fingers. That persistent temptation swept over him again. He would like to kiss her. He felt the muscles tighten along his arms and legs and over his shoulders. She was looking at him with soft affection. In that moment he knew that it was not scruples that held him back, but the fear of being rebuffed.

Under the friendly darkness he was crimson with emotion. He still held her hand. Suddenly with impulsive daring he bent his head and kissed it. Then with new and reckless courage he looked straight into her eyes, and said:

"Good-bye, Margie, sweetheart," and, turning, quickly left her.

He ventured another look when he was behind the wheel. She stood silhouetted against the light from the open door. Her left hand was over her head waving farewell and her right she held to her lips.

X

January and February at Kingston University was the open season for sophomores. To put it less colloquially, it was the period in which upper classmen called on sophomores and decided which to elect to their clubs. The elections came the first Monday in March when invitations arrived, or did not arrive, in the morning mail.

These ceremonies did not concern Davis directly this year, but he found quite an interest in seeing how the system worked.

"I don't think much of it," he pronounced after watching the proceedings for two weeks. "In the first place it sets false values on things and in the second it starts a lot of dirty politics among friends. Not to mention the fact that it's undemocratic and cruel to some people."

"I hope you don't think you're democratic," said Phil.

"Certainly I am."

"You think niggers and dagoes are just as good as you are, do you? You'd be perfectly willing to join a club with them?

"Well, I do draw the color line," admitted the democrat.

"And the race line and the religion line and the pedigree line and a few others."

Davis was confounded. "Anyhow, I don't go around telling people they're not as good as I am, and that's what this club system does."

"Sure it does, but if you know you're well up in the
65

upper division, what do you care? Nobody's going to tell you that."

"Don't you ever think about anyone but yourself, Phil?"

"I should say not. Why should I? Nobody else will if I don't."

"Where do you think you'd be today if nobody had thought about you?"

Tom raised his shaggy head from the sofa and said:
"He's got you there, Phil."

Tom took some pride in his roommate's wit, having little of his own.

"Got me where?" scoffed Phil. "I hope you don't still believe that parents write the stork a letter and ask for a baby boy to be nice to, do you? I don't think they do us any great favor getting us born. They ought to be fairly good to us after putting us to the trouble of living. Don't you suppose they get any selfish pleasure out of seeing us well dressed and fed? What would people say if we weren't?"

"You're just like Alvin Martin," said Davis, "you twist things around to suit yourself. What's all that got to do with the club system. I said it's cruel to some people and it is."

"Who said it wasn't?"

"Take this poor man Damp, for instance," Davis went on, ignoring the challenge. "He means well and really thinks he'll get in a club, although they seldom call on him. It'll be an awful jolt when he gets left out. A slap in the face. I call that cruel, and any system that stands for it is immoral."

"Hallelujah. Old Dave's getting pious again. I thought we had broken you of that.

"Joe," he greeted the new arrival with a flourish, "Joe, you're a good heathen. Will you join the S.P.C.D. Society for the Prevention of Cruelty to Damp?"

Joe opened his huge mouth and guffawed. He hurled his massive body upon the window seat and said:

"How about a little touch of something to drink before we swear in the new members?"

Davis became more conscious of it every day, this "estranging sea" which was isolating him from his old comrades. They did not understand his principles at all. To do them justice they did, especially Tom, make efforts to bring him around to what they considered a sensible point of view. Their new friends laughed at the queer person who roomed with Tom Stevenson, and Davis reciprocated by ignoring them with haughty contempt.

Being alone he spent much time and serious thought on his work. He took real interest in several of his courses and the professors seeing this, encouraged him. They asked him to call on them, lent him books and soon called him by his christian name.

Professor Redmond of history thought his receptive mind good ground in which to sow some of his own revolutionary and socialistic ideas. He showed Davis the injustices of capitalism, industrialism, and in fact of all organized government. He proved conclusively that the British Empire was the most tyranical organization since Rome, that all patriotism was submission to tyranny and all loyalty, pigheadedness. Mr. Harvey, atheist of the psychology department, took charge of his soul on questions of free will, predestination and sex, quoting him Freud, James and Schopenhauer. Old Doctor Down had him to dinner and sat up till two o'clock reading and discussing Keats, Shelley, Browning and Swinburne.

Davis felt that he was getting something out of college, whether Tom thought so or not. He reserved his opinion on some of the dicta of the radical pedagogues, but these new ideas worked on the walls of his dogma like an acid eating its way into steel.

As soon as he returned to Kingston he had written Margie, half-apologizing, half-belittling his emotional farewell. She had answered without mentioning it, and their correspondence went along as before; except that Davis began unconsciously to put into his letters some of his new feelings and ideas. His loneliness and discontent increased his tenderness towards her, and by February he decided to invite her to the prom on Washington's Birthday.

February twenty-second was a gala occasion at Kingston. It was Alumni Day and the university put forth its best efforts for the benefit of the returning graduates. Class exercises were suspended, there were several athletic contests and at night the prom would be held in the gymnasium.

Margie accepted with alacrity and joy. Davis set about making arrangements for her and her chaperone at the hotel. He looked forward to her visit with impatience. About a week before the great day, came a letter from Alvin. He was coming up for a reunion and wanted a bed for the night.

Davis met Margie at the station and, having discarded the chaperone at the hotel along with the luggage, escorted her about the campus with delicious pride. That evening after dinner with her Davis returned to his room to rest and dress for the dance.

Alvin was there lounging in the armchair. He, too, had spent a gay afternoon, not unmoistened by alcohol as Davis noticed as soon as he spoke. It was now eight o'clock; and there was no need to call for Margie till ten or ten-thirty, so they sat down to talk.

Alvin was very loquacious. He complained that none of his old chums had returned, just a lot of men whom he had never cared for at college.

"Even the Club isn't what it used it be. All the

real good ones married or reformed or dead. I hope you're feathering your nest for the elections next year. If you don't make the Owl, you miss half the fun of college."

"I don't think much of the crowd that's going there, Alvin. In my class they're a lot of rounders that do nothing but run to the city and break up night clubs."

"What do you expect them to do, stay here and play solitaire? Take my word for it, you don't want to be too good when you're young. A man's got to have his fling some time, and the longer you put it off the more you'll have to make up for lost time. Another thing! Don't bother about whether you like a man or not your first year. If you think he'll do you any good, cultivate him. I'll bet young Stevenson doesn't let them get away from him. He's not as dumb as he looks. And the Parsons boy, too. You get in behind him, and you won't go wrong."

"But suppose I think other things are more worth while?"

"Good God, boy, don't get serious-minded in freshman year. The longer you live the less you'll find is worth while. You take my word for it. I've been everywhere you've been, and back again."

Davis shook his head. It seemed everyone in the world was out of step but him.

"So you've got your girl up, have you? Well, she's not so bad, what's-her-name isn't. I used to have a great time at these proms. Like to have a nickel for every girl I've kissed up here. I wouldn't sell those kisses though for a million dollars each."

He clasped the nape of his neck and leaned back, stretching luxuriously.

"Margie's not that kind of girl," volunteered Davis, anxious to establish her divinity before Alvin made some impious remark.

"Not what kind?"

"Not the kissing kind. She's way above that."

Alvin snapped his mouth shut in the midst of a yawn.

"I always thought she was right good looking."

"Well, she is." Davis became suddenly cautious. He had seen Alvin lay his traps before.

"If she's good looking, she can be kissed. The only good girl is a homely one."

"Margie's different from most girls, I tell you. I know her and you don't."

Alvin snorted as he always did to convey contempt for another's opinion.

"Did you ever hear the little ditty that goes like this:

> 'O it's harder for me to be a bad girl
> Than for most girls to be good;
> I'd love to live in a mad whirl
> And I would if I could.
> I'd love to sit in a corner
> With someone to hug and to kiss,
> But it's harder for me to be a bad girl
> With a goddam face like this.' "

Davis flared up, his eyes glaring.

"That's not as funny as you think," he said.

Alvin's mood became serious.

"Now, Davis, I didn't mean to hurt your feelings, but you're a perfect child to have such ideas. I know a man who's been an unhappy bachelor all his life because he had ideas like that."

"What happened to him?" Davis accepted the apology gruffly.

"The same thing that's going to happen to you if you don't take good advice. Now stop huffing or I won't tell you."

He tilted the reading lamp so that it did not shine

in his eyes and leisurely lit a cigarette. Davis sat waiting for the story and tried to look less hostile.

"Well, this man was in my class at college. He was what you would call a rounder. He liked the liquor and he kissed the girls. But all of a sudden he fell in love with a girl that fooled him. She told him she was different and he believed it. He went simply mad over her, sighed and carried on like a perfect ass. He thought she was too good to be kissed, too holy to be touched and so he stood off and worshiped her. The girl loved him too, but girls don't love as men do. They are like a machine gun nest. As long as you stand off and make motions at them they pepper you; but if you rush in, they're not good at close range and easy enough to capture. And they like to be captured. Don't make any mistake about that.

"Well this poor chap didn't know it. He loved her so much he forgot she was just like all the other girls he had kissed. He hung around getting shot to pieces until pretty soon another man came along, rushed the nest and carried away the girl that was different. Consequently my friend's a crusty old bachelor today and perfectly miserable because he knows she loves him still. But, of course, it's too late now."

He made as if to end the tale; but then quickly went on, suddenly changing his mood from the serious to his characteristic banter.

"Therein lies the moral, young man. Get it out of your head that it's indecent of a girl to want to be kissed. Haven't you ever wanted to kiss Margie?"

"No," he lied gallantly.

"Then you're not in love with her."

"Even if I have—"

"Oh, I thought so. Just you remember that when you feel that way she does too. Also remember this; if you don't, someone else will."

Davis went to his bedroom and began to undress, leaving the door open. He saw Alvin throw away his cigarette and stare moodily at the floor. An idea flashed into his mind, and he wondered that he had not thought of it before.

"Alvin, how come you never married?" he asked, not tauntingly, but kindly.

Alvin started out of his revery and snorted.

"Imagine getting married while there are races to ride. That reminds me, Davis, how would you like to ride your first race this spring?"

"How would I? There's nothing I'd like more."

"Not even to kiss that girl?"

Davis laughed good naturedly now.

"Well, that's telling," he said. "But how about this race?"

"I thought if you really wanted to begin racing I'd see you get a good start. There's that race at Madingly on Easter Monday. Maybe I'll put you up on old Johnnie Walker; he won it last year."

"That's mighty kind of you, Alvin, but don't you want to ride yourself?"

"Certainly I do, but I'll have plenty other rides. Is it a bargain?"

"Sold," said Davis.

On his way to Margie's hotel Davis Pettigrier was thoughtful. He had heard so much lately of the theory Alvin had been expounding. Professor Harvey had dealt with the matter impersonally and scientifically, Phil Parsons was always quoting practical examples from his own experience. After all, if a man was in love with a girl why shouldn't he kiss her or why shouldn't she want to be kissed by a man she loved? Of course that was assuming that Margie did love him—which he had to admit with quite an assumption. But this was a good way to find out, urged one voice, and to seal the bargain on the spot. Also, said another voice, a good chance to spoil everything, better to let events take their course. Suddenly he reminded himself that he was completely forgetting that Margie was different. He was ashamed of himself. He was letting people like Alvin, Phil and Professor Harvey lead him astray. Why, not one of these even believed in God. How could they understand a divine creature like Margie? Anyone could see with half an eye that God existed and with the other half that Margie was an angel.

But the first voice would not be still until he entered the lobby and found her waiting for him. He was late and very sorry.

Margie was clad in a blue dress that stopped abruptly at the knees. It was tight fitting and scant. There was none of the romance of antiquity about her that there had been the last time Davis had seen her in evening clothes. Now she was dressed as all the other girls at the prom would be. He was not disappointed. How could he be when she rose and came forward to meet him with that irresistible smile and manner?

At the prom Davis found to his dismay that the few friends he had were not nearly enough to give her a good time. Desperately he sought Tom and found him down in the locker rooms drinking out of a flask. His new set was clustered about him and Davis hesitated to force himself upon them. Tom, however, caught his eye and called him. Davis accepted a drink from the flask, and was displeased when he found that it belonged to Bob Johnson, whom he had consistently ignored.

"How about helping me out with Margie, Tom? I want to give her a good time, but I don't know many people here."

"Sure, Dave, I will. Look, you-all, there's a regular southern beauty upstairs just waiting to meet you."

"I'm first," said Johnson.

Davis turned away. He hated the idea of this person putting his arm around Margie's waist. He had let himself in for a bad evening, he feared.

Tom introduced his friends and they their friends. Margie became the belle of the ball, so much so that Davis spent most of his time sulking in a corner watching stranger after stranger hold her hand and encircle her waist.

When supper time came, she came up on Tom's arm and Tom said, "Be a sport, Dave, and let me take her to supper. You've had her all day."

Margie was neutral.

"Toss you for it," Davis compromised. He lost and his spirits dropped still lower. He decided he was not hungry, and in sheer despair drifted back to his room. Alvin was asleep on the sofa but he awoke when Davis absentmindedly switched on the light.

"Oh, I beg your pardon, Alvin. I swear I forgot all about your being there. Why don't you take my bed? I won't be needing it till you're ready for breakfast."

"What's wrong with you? Where's your girl?"

"Haven't got a girl," said Davis tragically, "she's too damn popular."

Alvin sat up and lit a cigarette while the dejected young man slumped into a chair.

"Well, I've never seen a race won by that kind of riding. You ought to be down at the gym making your run instead of moping around here. What's the idea?"

"Tom's having supper with her."

"He'll be having breakfast with her too if you let him. Why did you let him?"

"Oh, I don't know."

"You don't know anything and you refuse to learn.

I told you that if you didn't do something someone else would, and here you are sitting around waiting for them to do it."

"I know Tom wouldn't do me like that."

"Davis, you idiot, no man is to be trusted in matters of that sort. Especially if he's got a drink or so in him."

Davis remembered the flask and the company Tom was keeping.

"Tom knows how I feel, more or less, and he wouldn't. I'll swear to it."

Not wanting to keep Alvin awake he soon took his departure, and wandered over the campus shivering with cold and boiling with jealousy.

Finally he returned to the gymnasium. Supper was over and the music had started again. He could find neither of the pair he had left together. He walked round and round the floor till his legs ached numbly and his eyes were throbbing. Alvin's warning he could not forget. He decided to go out and get a breath of air. In the doorway he met Tom and Margie coming in.

"We took a walk," she said.

"Nice long walk," answered Davis sourly.

"I'm sorry, Dave," Tom apologized, "I didn't think you would mind and I really forgot how long it was."

He surrendered Margie to Davis and took her cloak, while the latter led her to the floor and began dancing.

"Davis, why are you so angry? I hadn't seen him for ever so long, and he wanted to tell me about his new girl in Philadelphia. You went away yourself and so after we'd had supper we just took a walk. You act as if we were a couple of criminals."

"It's all right, Margie. I'm not mad at all, I was just worried not knowing where you were. Will you sit out with me a little later?"

She nodded. Davis caught sight of Johnson weav-

ing through the dancers with the evident intention of
cutting in. When he felt the hand on his elbow, Davis
turned away in disgust, but not quickly enough to miss
hearing Johnson say flippantly to her:

"Well, how are you-all now?"

Later on Davis claimed the privilege of sitting out
with her. She put on her cloak and they went out. It
was a cool night, but not cold for February. It felt
fresh and invigorating after the stale air indoors.
They breathed great lungfuls of it and forgot they
were tired and sleepy. It was almost four o'clock.

At Margie's suggestion they got into a car that was
parked near-by. He was still thinking of what Alvin
had said. The two voices were debating within him
and he was again telling them to be quiet, that there
was no question of policy involved, that Margie was
different.

"Margie, do you remember when I told you good-
bye last Christmas? Did you think I was crazy?"

"No, Davis, why should I?"

"Because I was crazy—about someone."

She was silent now and played with a ribbon on
her dress.

"Do you remember what I called you then?"

"No, what? Tell me again."

"I called you sweetheart. Did you mind?"

"No, Davis."

"Margie sweetheart."

It came so easily, so naturally and yet so softly that
he wondered if she heard. She did hear and looked
at him with eyes languid in expectation.

"I've loved you since I first saw you in church, even
before I knew your name."

Unwittingly he touched her hand, which lay on the
seat between them. He ran his fingers caressingly over
it and when she did not remove it clasped it in his own.

"Davis," she always called him by his full name

when she was serious, "do you really love me, or are you like the others, just making love for a conquest?"

It sounded to him like a rebuke, and he let loose her hand and faced her squarely.

"Margie, I love you better than my own soul, better than God even. I know you aren't like other girls. You're different and I love you differently. I love you for yourself, your soul, and not your body. The way I feel is so far beyond the physical that it sounds sacrilegious even to mention it. But I want you to know, Margie, I think you're perfect. I worship the ground you tread and the air you breathe."

He stopped, moved and breathless at his own eloquence.

"Oh, Davis, Davis, if ever I should disappoint you. I'm not that good, really."

"Margie, of course you are, and I love you all the more for saying you're not."

There were no voices arguing within him now. All was deep, blissful peace.

They sat on for half an hour, but he had said all he had to say and the spell was broken. They talked in affectionate tones of commonplace matters, and went back to the dance, each determined not to suggest going home till it was over.

The prom lasted till six, and the crowd of weary revelers walked or rode to different restaurants for breakfast. It was eight when Davis entered his own room, and found Alvin fresh and ruddy from his cold shower and on the point of departing. Tom had not come in yet.

"Well, look at this."

Davis laughed with the jubilance that the dawn gives to a tired dancer.

"What's more, you look as if you had finally taken good advice."

"Alvin, it gives me the greatest of pleasure to say,

'I told you so.' For once in my life I'm right and you're wrong."

"Meaning she admitted she was different."

"Meaning I proved it."

"I reckon you're hopeless. Well, I'm catching an early train for Boston. Things happening for all concerned since the Lucases came to town. Thanks for putting me up, old boy. See you at Easter and don't forget about the race."

"No chance of that, Alvin. So long."

XI

The last week in February was also the last week of club calling. Sophomores stood about in nervous groups talking over their hopes and misgivings. Upper classmen looked wise and made evasive answers to all questions. Poor Damp sat alone in his room or scurried from lecture to lecture like a timid child doing errands after dark. He had no friends to talk prospects with, nor prospects to discuss even if he had.

Tom admitted in private that it was a sad case, but in the presence of his chosen associates he mimicked Damp's stutter and laughed at Davis' sympathy.

"I tell you he doesn't know what it's all about, Dave. You might as well pity a worm for getting its belly dirty."

Davis knew that the comparison was not of Tom's origin. It was all Tom could do to remember things other people said, let alone make up expressions of his own.

He went into Damp's room now and then and tried to make light conversation, but these visits were very trying. One thing he was thankful for, that Damp never talked of his own plight nor pitied himself. They never mentioned clubs to one another.

He found out Damp's christian name was Richard, called him Dick, and was repaid tenfold for the ragging he took from Tom by the tacit appreciation he got from the object of pity. The only bad effects of these visits were that Damp began to repay them. This made Tom furious and Davis feared that some time he would insult the poor fellow.

When Tom voiced his objection Davis replied, "I don't like your friends any better than you like mine.

You be careful how you treat him or I'll have something to say myself."

"At least my friends are gentlemen. I should think that would make some difference to you. It wouldn't hurt you to be more of a snob."

"If you ask me I should say your friends have more money than blood. As far as I can see that's what makes a gentleman up this way, money. And as for being a snob, I don't have to be."

"Well, it all depends on what generation made the money; just because some great, great grandfather of yours made it—"

"Where did you pick up that old argument? I know you didn't do it yourself."

"Well, what of it? All I got to say is; keep that scum out of here or he'll get his feelings hurt, if he has any."

Davis did try to keep him out by every means but frankness and rudeness.

The first Monday in March came and the postman was besieged by anxious, desperate sophomores. He refused to disobey orders by giving mail out of turn. Some of the anxious ones followed him from room to room till he came to their own. Others sought friends who had received their mail, in hopes of getting some early news.

Davis sat on the window seat and watched the postman circle the court, stopping at every entry. He was hoping for a letter from Margie. The official entered the hall outside the door. The letter slot flipped open and shut and a blue envelope dropped through on to the carpet. Eagerly he picked it up, but as he stood there he heard Damp's door open and Damp's voice ask:

"Anything for me?"

"Nothing but this here paper."

It was inevitable, thought Davis; how could the

poor chap have expected an invitation? He sat down
to read his own letter, but before he had removed the
envelope he heard two persons enter the hall, and by
their voices recognized Tom and Johnson.

"Hello, Damp, did you get an Owl bid? I wouldn't
accept it, if I were you, there's a rotten crowd going
there this year."

It was Johnson who said this, and Tom who laughed
at it. As they came in Davis saw Damp standing by his
own open door holding a rolled up newspaper in his
hand.

Davis shoved the letter into his pocket and advanced
towards the other two.

"Johnson, you low-down dog you, you dirty cad,
get out of this room before I throw you out."

Johnson, being fully twenty pounds heavier, did not
seem moved by the threat, but the appellations seemed
to sting. Before he could answer, Tom Stevenson,
crimson with rage, had stepped between them.

"That'll be enough out of you, Pettigrier. If you
haven't got the manners of a gentleman, by God, I'll
teach you."

"You won't do anything, Stevenson, and I know it.
I mean the same of you I said of him. You're a pair
of dirty cads and not half the men or gentlemen that
fellow across the hall is. That was the cruelest thing
I ever heard anyone doing. Now get out of here, Johnson. You heard me."

"If he goes, I go with him and I don't come back.
I'm sick of you anyhow."

Davis winced at this, but said defiantly, "That suits
me. I'm damn sick of you, too."

Johnson went to the door and jerked it open.

"Let's go, Tom. I'd never have come if I'd known
this prig would be here."

They stamped out and slammed the door on a man

who had severed a life-long friendship for the sake of
an abstract ideal.

Davis crossed the hall, tapped on the door, and entered without waiting for an answer. Damp was standing by the table still holding the paper.

"Hello, Dick, got any new records?"

He went to the victrola and turned over some discs.

"No, nothing nu-new, Dave."

His heart went out to this man who swallowed his
bitterness so bravely. They sat and talked of small
matters and played a few pieces. When it was lunch
time Davis suggested they go together, a thing he had
never done before.

In the restaurant several people looked at the strange
pair. They both pretended not to notice. Joe and
Phil came in, nodded, but did not seem to see the two
empty places there and took another table in a distant
corner.

After luncheon Damp said he had an engagement
and left. Davis joined his two friends.

"I'll take it back, Dave, you are getting democratic,
but if I were you I wouldn't be so dramatic about it."

"I know you wouldn't, Phil. Don't think I want to
be either, but this has been a bad day for him."

"It'll be a bad day for you if you're going to make
that gesture a precedent. There's such a thing as
common sense, you know."

"I wouldn't be seen with that guy in a subway,"
said Joe Watson, chuckling over a huge plate of steak
and fried potatoes. "Let alone in a respectable
restaurant."

"Seen Tom?" asked Davis.

They had not.

"He's in a tantrum. Swears he'll never come in the
room again. All because of Damp, too."

"Dave," said Phil, "I don't suppose there's any use
arguing with you; you're always right. But take it

from me you're making a fool of yourself. You'll be sorry to lose friends like Tom."

"I know I will, Phil. I don't want to, either, but I lose my temper when people don't do what I think is right; and Tom's got a temper, too."

Joe pushed back his plate, and called to the waiter for some strawberry short cake.

"Tell you what, Dave. I can fix it with Tom. I didn't room with him three years for nothing. But it won't do any good to patch it up if you're going to keep on like this."

The short cake arrived and Joe transferred two heaping fork loads to his mouth before going on.

"If you promise me you'll ease up on Damp, and try to be decent to other people, and come to the city with us now and then; and stop acting like a damn—"

Here his articulation was smothered by several more cubic inches of food and he swallowed with difficulty, saying:

"Like a damn-you-know-what-I-mean."

"Hermit," suggested Phil.

Davis picked some crumbs from the table and heaped them up into a miniature snow pile. The last thing he wanted was an open break with Tom, but neither did he wish to buy back his friendship.

Phil sat looking at his own long nervous fingers spread out on the table.

"You know, Dave, you've been just as intolerant of our ideas and friends as we have of yours. We don't pretend to be virtuous, but you do, and tolerance is a great virtue."

"I know, Phil. I'm sorry I've been such a prig. I'll try to be better, but I really can't make any unqualified statements."

"But you'll promise to try? All right then," said Joe, "I'll see Tom. I can fix it all up between you. Waiter, bring me another glass of milk, please."

Davis went back to his room and waited for Tom. About five o'clock Joe came.

"He says nothing doing, unless you apologize to Johnson."

"All right, you tell him I will when Johnson apologizes to Damp."

Joe sat down heavily on the sofa.

"I thought you promised to stop acting like that."

"That's all I've got to say. You don't know what happened, do you?"

"Yes, he told me. I must say it was pretty mean of Johnson, but Tom can't help that. All he did was laugh. Well, I've done my best. I'll tell him, but it won't do any good. I've got to be going. By the way, can I borrow your chemistry problems after you've done them?"

When he had left, Davis remembered the letter in his pocket.

"Dear Davis," wrote Margie, "first I want to thank you for the wonderful time I had at the prom. You were sweet to have me.

"What I want to say most is that I think you're the most wonderful person I've ever known. I think your ideals and everything are perfectly splendid. I hope you will never lower your standards, but, Davis, you must not think too highly of me. I am only human, after all, and I'm so afraid someday I'll do something to disappoint you.

"I hope we shall always care for each other as we do now. I have never had a brother and I look upon you as the only one I'll ever have.

"When I got back to school I was so tired—"

"A brother," thought Davis, and thrilled at the word. "That means she loves me."

He went to the moving pictures that night alone and returning to his room before ten o'clock, sat down to work for an hour or so before retiring. About ten-thirty the door opened and Tom walked in. Davis controlled his joy with difficulty.

Tom shut the door and said proudly, "I've come for clothes. Tomorrow I'll move everything down to Bob's room."

"You're really leaving for good, Tom?"

"I told you so this morning, and as long as you refused to apologize this afternoon, I don't see anything else to do."

"You said this morning you were sick of me, so I suppose you might as well go; I'll get a single room next term and you-all can take this."

Tom went into his bedroom to pack; and Davis, not anxious to stand and watch him and quite willing to leave a defiant impression, went across the hall to Damp's room.

Knocking and entering as before, he found the room dark. He felt for the electric button and pressed it. Damp was sitting on a straight chair drawn up to the table. His forehead was resting on the table, his hands were clenched and his arms were stretched out before him. Near his right hand was a glass discolored by the remains of some fluid.

"Dick," said Davis weakly. There was something ominous in the sight. He went up and shook him by the shoulder. The head rolled sideways and Davis, who had never seen a dead man before, knew that he was touching one now.

For one moment he felt paralyzed and the next as if he wanted to scream. He did not scream, however, but walked quickly back to his own room and called Tom.

Together they went back. Tom said, "Good God!" and turned pale. Then Davis noticed an envelope on the table addressed to himself. He tore it open and read:

"Dear Dave: You are the only one I could possibly write to. I want to thank you for all you've done for me. Don't think I don't understand, because I do. I realized that before long you, too, would go your own way and now I have chosen mine. It's been the same all my life and this is for the best as far as I'm concerned. I know when I've had enough.

"Would it be too much to ask you to drop in and see my mother some time. Tell her you knew me and we were friends. The address is 1442 John Street, Waketown, Pennsylvania.

"So long.   Dick."

"I suppose we ought to go for the proctors, don't you think, Tom?"

"Yes," said Tom, clearing his throat, "I suppose so."

CHAPTER XII

Tom did not change rooms. He seemed so humbled that he scarcely met his roommate's eye for the next two weeks. Johnson wrote Davis a note of abject apology.

"You were right," his note ran, "I was a dirty cad. Nothing I can say will tell you how I feel about it all."

At the coroner's inquest Davis said only that Richard Damp had seemed particularly depressed that day. The jury learned that the liquid was composed of several deadly chemicals which the deceased had taken from the chemistry laboratory that afternoon. They learned also that the deceased's late father had had an insane uncle. They turned in a verdict of suicide due to temporary insanity.

Davis went to Waketown for the funeral, and found the mother rather what he expected. The visit was very depressing, for Mrs. Damp wept and cried that she was all alone in the world and begged him not to leave her.

When he returned to Kingston, he was moody and thoughtful. For three days he mentioned nothing connected with the tragedy; then one day when the four friends were together in his room he burst out:

"I said so before and I repeat it. This whole system is rotten and cruel and immoral. The whole thing put together isn't worth the life of one human being. It isn't worth the lacerated feelings or the terrible sufferings it brings to people year after year. I hate the whole thing and I'm going to fight it as long as I'm here. I won't join a club myself, and I'll get every honest man in the class to stay out with me as a protest."

87

Joe and Tom looked at Phil simultaneously as if to appoint him their spokesman.

"Now, Dave, look here," said Phil. "You've got to see it from a reasonable point of view. Every kind of competition is cruel in a way. Neither you nor anyone else can make things come out even for everyone. There's such a thing as compensation, but you can't regulate it; and what's the use of butting a stone wall? You only hurt yourself."

"He's right, Dave, you only hurt yourself butting a stone wall."

"That's an easy way to shirk all duties, just say, 'what's the use? I can't do any good.' How do you suppose reforms are ever made?"

"It really isn't as important as all that," said Joe.

"Human life and happiness aren't important? Then what is?"

No one answered and Davis went on.

"I don't intend to ask any of you to help. You're too selfish. You-all know you won't be left out and don't care about anyone else."

"What are you going to do?"

"First I'm going to write editorials to the *Campus* and sign my name. They'll have to print them."

He wrote his first one later that night. It was a wild and bitter protest, built on a solid structure of humanitarianism and reason. A few days later it was printed over his name.

The next day came an answer, sneering and cavilling at the writer's nonsense. Davis wrote another. This time he quoted facts without names. He told anecdotes of how friends had deserted one another; had done what amounted to blackmail, in order to get in a fashionable club. He told how the clubs had fought among themselves for the most desirable candidates and resorted to any number of dishonorable means.

He ended by challenging anyone to dare him to give names.

This created a mild stir, but when a New York paper published an interview with Davis Pettigrier covering practically the same points, the whole university, official and undergraduate, rose in indignation. The dean sent for Davis and asked him what he meant by giving Kingston a black eye. Davis asked him in turn if he did not think a college that fostered such a black organization as the club system needed a black eye to match. The dean called it impertinence; and Davis proved, before he could open his mouth again, that any system that caused one death a year might just as well cause two or two hundred. The dean ended the interview abruptly, and the next morning at breakfast read it almost verbatim in a New York paper.

A committee of seniors called on Davis and challenged him to show them any feasible system that would not hurt somebody's feelings. Davis went to his desk, brought out several sheets of paper, and read them a constitution he had drawn up. It made the clubs practically hotels where anyone who paid could eat and sleep. The committee stamped out of the room. The morning paper contained this interview and printed Davis' reform bill.

He became a prominent figure on the campus. He was pointed out in the lecture rooms and stared at in the restaurants. A motley crowd of non-club members gathered about their new champion, but the rest of the university snubbed him as an upstart and a rebel.

Down in Cranston Mr. Pettigrier was worried. He had always hoped Davis would be a leader of men, but he took no pride in his son's present rôle. He stopped off at Kingston to talk it over. Davis became so worked up in discussing it that he wept from sheer nervous excitement.

The father was all the more upset by this and suggested that Davis take a week at home to rest. This the young man absolutely refused to do.

After two weeks the intensity began to lessen. Answers to his editorials became desultory, even patronizing; and Davis wisely let the matter drop, vowing to take it up again before the elections next year.

He had now identified himself with a definite group, the non-club members, the outcasts of the university. Individually they were much on the Damp order, slovenly, insipid, unattractive. It irked Davis, last of the Pettigriers, to be forced into such company, but manfully he called them brothers for the sake of his ideals.

For a few weeks Tom was very kind and indulgent. He was even condescendingly polite to the queer persons who came to see Davis. But as Time drew its curtain closer about the tragedy across the hall Tom became more and more his own self. He took his books to other rooms to study in the evenings. He went to the city with his selected friends, and when the term came to its close the relationship between the roommates, though not openly hostile, was strained.

XIII

Standing before the electric stove, his brown, trimly cut suit hanging perfectly from his square shoulders and narrow loins, his keen gray eyes lighted with tenderness, and the corners of his strong mouth twitching with humor, no one could justly deny that Alvin Martin was a handsome man. Indeed, there was nobody there to deny it, for surely the lady seated on the sofa before him would never do so, and they were the only two present.

"Alvin, do you know I worry a lot about your religion?"

"Didn't know I had any to worry about."

"That's just it. I'm a wicked woman, but I have religion. I couldn't do without it."

"You're wicked with religion and I'm wicked without it. Which is worse?"

"Don't you really believe in God at all? Who do you think makes the grass grow?"

"Some call it Nature and others call it God. Certainly I believe in God, but not the Father-which-art-in-heaven kind. That's absurd. Why, an earthly father wouldn't let his children suffer as human beings do."

"Maybe God can't help it."

"Then he isn't God. Yes, I believe in a God, all right, but most people call him Fate. He isn't a Father, but he's a King. No one on earth has any say-so about anything important. Circumstance rules us all."

"Maybe God doesn't see all the suffering on earth.

There's so much due to sin, you know, and sin ought to be punished."

"But there's no guarantee that a good man will be happy or a bad man unhappy. It may happen either way. I'll tell you a story that illustrates exactly my belief in Fate or God."

"Oh, you and your stories! Go ahead."

"Last spring I went to Maryland to ride a race. I'd never seen the horse I was to ride, but the owner swore to me he was a sure winner. Well, I've ridden bad actors, but never one like this. He put his head down at the drop of the flag and started to run, pulling like a train. Didn't bother to jump the fences, just ran through them; and the funny thing was he didn't seem to know how to fall any better than he knew how to jump. He'd hit a fence, slide half way into the next one on his knees, get up and do it again. I was scared to death and wished he would fall so I could get off.

"Finally he did, at a fence coming down hill. Turned completely over, landing on me and the saddle. I got up feeling like an ironed shirt and was wondering whether there was any use getting back on, when a darky groom ran up, grabbed the bridle and said:

" 'Boss, don't get on that horse again. He ain't blind, sir, he just don't give a damn!'

"That's what I believe about Fate. I don't believe it's malicious especially, just indifferent, 'just don't give a damn'."

"Oh, Alvin, you can't believe all that. Don't you think man has any will or power over his own destiny? What's the use of trying then, what can we do about it?"

"That's only my theory, Tommie. Go to those wiser than I for an answer. You can get any number of them." He waved his hand toward the shelves of books. "Some say it is written that the hairs of your head are numbered and that neither the darkness of night nor the wings of the morning can save you from Fate. Your Philosopher says that if Fate slaps you on one cheek, you should turn the other and sing hymns praising his love and mercy. Another says, 'At least we'll die with harness on our back.' Still another says to take a book and a jug of wine into the wilderness and wait for death. Personally I believe in the one who said:

> " 'In the fell clutch of circumstance
> I have not winced nor cried aloud;
> Under the bludgeonings of chance
> My head is bloody but unbowed.'

"Not very good poetry, but damn good philosophy."

"Don't talk like that, Alvin."

"You mean God might try to strike me with lightning and hit you instead?"

Laughing he sat down beside her and passed his arm about her waist.

"He'll have to take us both if he does, Tommie."

She pouted and snuggled against his shoulder.

"Do you remember when you started calling me Tommie?"

"When we used to climb trees together. I called you tomboy and then Tommie. I don't believe anyone else has ever heard me call you that, I only do when we're alone."

"Oh, Alvin, why didn't I marry you? We could have been so happy and needn't to have hidden away like this."

"I never asked you, that's why," he said banteringly.

"You were afraid to. You thought I might not accept. I don't believe I would have, either. Mother didn't like you. She said you drank and were 'wild'."

"You wouldn't have minded your mother if you'd loved me. You didn't then and I know why, because I never kissed you and the other one did. You fell in love with him and couldn't get married quickly enough."

"But I love you now. I did then, too, and didn't know it."

"Tommie, I hate this whole business. We're worse than sinners, we're traitors. He's my friend and your husband. Some day I'm going away and not coming back. Why couldn't I have kept on loving you the way I did for years?"

"There's no such thing as 'pure' love, Alvin, if you mean so-called platonic love."

"There is for a man. I loved you just as much before I ever kissed you. I wish I still loved you that way."

"Alvin, with all your cynicism you're as innocent as a child. Don't you know that passion is as inevitable as food and sleep? You can't blame yourself for that."

"When I commit a sin, I call it a sin, and don't try to convince myself otherwise. It's absurd the way people treat sex nowadays, saying it's a necessity, when it's only a luxury. Just because they don't want to resist it they say it's irresistible. It's utter nonsense and I don't know what the world is coming to."

In his fervor he had risen and was facing the door with his hands deep in his pockets. She laughed a genuine laugh of amusement.

"Imagine anyone hearing you attacking modern immorality."

"I never mentioned immorality. I mean modern hypocrisy. When I was young we didn't call wild oats the staff of life."

"Alvin, come and sit down. I've something much

more serious to talk about. I think certain people suspect us."

"Good God, Tommie—"

"Yes, old Mrs. MacGregor looked very wise this afternoon when I declined her dinner saying I had to go slumming."

"That settles it. I'm going away. I can buy a partnership in Baltimore. I can't let you suffer on my account."

"Now, Alvin, calm down. Nothing is known yet; and besides, why should we care what people like that think? If I don't, surely, you shouldn't. And if you loved me you wouldn't even think of leaving. I'm the one who has something to lose. It's the woman who pays."

He came over and took her hand.

"Dearest Tommie, you know I love you better than myself."

She drew him down beside her and kissed him, holding his head in both arms against her bosom. Meekly he retracted all his threats and swore never to desert her as long as they lived. Then she put on her wraps and left.

Alvin sat alone in thought. He wondered how women hold such power over strong men. He had never wanted this intrigue. After she married he only wanted to love her, to worship her as he always had. She had practically forced him into sin, coming to his study when he begged her to stay away, thwarting his own plan to leave the community. Grimly he asked himself how the impression became prevalent that men seduce women. He had never been happy in these circumstances. He despised himself for deceiving his good friend, who was also her devoted husband. Formerly he had suffered like a martyr, but now like a criminal.

XIV

When Davis returned to Cranston on Monday of
Holy Week he behaved and felt like a soldier back
from the wars. He was gaunt and drawn. He looked
on familiar sights and places with a tired and loving
eye. Home and the homefolk had never seemed so
sweet. The warm, young air of a southern spring
blew on the puckered forehead and soothed the aching
brain.

"He'll pick up quickly now he's away from all that
tomfoolery up there," said the anxious father. "What
he needs is plenty of rest and good food. For the
Lord's sake, Molly, let's don't start any argument
with him. He's had too many already. I'll speak to
Alvin about it."

"Did Alvin tell you he'd asked Davis to ride his
horse in a race?"

"No, he didn't say anything to me. I think he
might have. When did he tell you; while I was
away?"

"I didn't see him while you were gone. It must
have been yesterday and you weren't listening."

Mr. Pettigrier met Alvin at the club that night.

"What's all this about Davis and Johnnie Walker?
You might have told me, Alvin. Those races are
dangerous and I don't want that boy broken up. He's
home for a rest."

"I thought I'd let him tell you," said Alvin. "I
didn't want to get Molly on my back, but I didn't
think you'd mind."

"Molly said you told her."

"I did nothing of the sort. Well, now, maybe I did.

I ran into her while you were away and it slipped out. Anyhow, what's the objection? Even if he does fall it won't hurt him. Does a man good to hit the ground now and then. These young fellows are too soft, too pampered."

"It's a dangerous game and you know it, Alvin. Why do they have an ambulance on the course if it isn't?"

"You don't think it's dangerous to live in your house just because there's fire insurance on it, do you?"

"No sense arguing with these smart lawyers, Jackson," put in Louis Davis, who overheard; "they can do you out of your life, wife and alimony."

That evening at dinner Mr. Pettigrier said: "Davis, I'm giving a little luncheon party for you Easter Monday at the club. Don't make any other engagements."

Davis looked up from his plate in dismay.

"All right, father, only I did have an engagement; but it doesn't matter."

"If it isn't important, you'd better make it for Tuesday."

"All right, father," he said, and was about to return half-heartedly to his dinner when he heard Mr. Pettigrier chuckle.

"I tried to call your bluff, son, but you stuck to it. Why didn't you tell us about your other engagement before?"

"I was going to break it Easter day, because I wasn't sure how you-all would take it; and then it would be almost too late to change."

"I didn't know you were taught deception at Kingston, Davis," said his mother. "You hurt me very much, deceiving your father and me like that."

"Well, Molly, don't suppose we're all perfect in small things, it's the big things that count."

"Jackson, I can't understand you treating it so lightly. If Davis learns to deceive when he's young—"

"Yes, Molly, but you're a good woman and don't understand how little white lies and so forth will slip out. Women are higher beings than men. Women don't know how to be dishonest. I remember my mother, she was the soul of honor, just like you, Molly."

Jackson Pettigrier smiled at his beautiful wife. Then, turning on his son and trying to be stern, he said:

"Now, sir, don't let this happen again. I hope I can see you ride. By gad, wouldn't it be great if you won! But, no, I forgot, I must go to the directors' luncheon and make a speech."

By Alvin's orders Davis rose every morning at six during Holy Week and together they drove out to where Johnnie Walker was training.

The last five days before the race it was Davis whom the trainer tossed into the saddle and to whom he gave orders about the distance and speed he was to go.

Johnnie Walker was a beautiful model of a small horse, with the neat, trim lines of a thoroughbred, but in physique he looked to horsemen too frail for a first-class point-to-pointer. This made it all the more remarkable that his record was better than any horse's in the community. People gave the credit to Alvin and said that nobody else could get such results out of Johnnie Walker.

Alvin always rose in praise and defense of his silent partner. The little horse was the pride of his heart. If there was blame, he took it; if there was praise, it all went to Johnnie Walker.

Saturday morning after they had paid their final visit to the training stables Alvin and Davis drove to Madingly in order to walk the course.

Alvin delivered a lecture of instructions, advice

and warning the whole way round. Davis was to
ease up over this hill, was to jump such and such a
panel, was under no circumstances to do that, and was,
for God's sake, to remember this and this and that.

The fences were alarmingly big and stiff. The
course seemed to offer every chance of doing something wrong. Suppose he cut a flag, refused a jump,
fell, was badly hurt! Or even worse, suppose he injured Johnnie Walker! "Good Lord," thought Davis,
and wished he had not wanted to be heroic. Why had
he not been content to stand on the ground and watch
others take chances, men like Alvin, who really were
of heroic stuff, and not a shaking, quaking coward
like himself? But he was in for it now and there
·was no way out. Silently he listened and nodded to
all Alvin said.

Mrs. Lucas had, with great condescension, allowed
Margie to accept his invitation to drive to Madingly.

"Of course," she had said, "it was never done in
my day, and I wouldn't permit it with any other
person but you, Davis. I trust you, but I'll be what
John always says if I trust many of these modern
boys—or girls either," wheeling on Margie.

Davis had assured her that he fully appreciated her
faith and would try to deserve it.

"Try, young man, try? Don't talk to me about trying. I've seen young people try before. Margie always tries to get home early from dances and tries
to remember, and tries to behave. I don't want any
trying. You make very certain of all I said or I'll
·come along myself and then I know it'll be all right."

"Yes, ma'am," Davis had agreed.

This had all occurred on Saturday, and on Monday
morning as he drove to town, using the old railroad
crossing that he and Tom had used when first he

called on Margie, Davis was a little fearful that Mrs. Lucas might have changed her feminine mind.

Having long since dropped the formality of the doorbell, Davis walked in, looked first in the living-room, then the dining-room. He discovered only a maid and inquired for Miss Margie. At the sound of his voice came another from the upper regions, and soon following it came its lovely owner.

She was dressed in brown and carried a cape over her arm.

"I've got a surprise for you. Look."

She held up the cape and turned it around. It was blue with a white collar and lining—his colors.

"I had it made specially for the occasion, and, Davis, will you carry my favor for good luck?" She gave him a snapshot of herself.

Davis felt numbly happy. Speech and thought for the moment were not within his power. And yet if he could have remained thus forever, speechless and thoughtless, he would have done so. But lives are not so ordered that men can preserve the great moments and dismiss the ordinary. In another instant Mrs. Lucas had surrounded them by a quick sortie from the kitchen. She bore a lunch basket on her arm.

"Now, Davis, no trying, understand, and don't let Margie try either. I don't trust her an inch, I pin all my faith on you and—well, I declare, Margie, the last thing I told you was not to forget your over-shoes. See that? She tried to remember. I'll wager she forgot something else I told her to put on, too. I'd better run up and see."

So saying, the mother followed her daughter up-stairs, to the deep embarrassment of the latter. In five minutes they both returned, one still suspicious, the other still abashed.

The young pair set off. What they talked about those thirty miles is not known, but when Roswell

Schnell saw them eating lunch at the course he was impressed by their mutual good humor.

Roswell Schnell could not see from where he sat in his blue roadster that Margie's escort was as a matter of fact eating very little. Davis, in spite of the long drive and the brisk April day, found that he was not hungry; found that chicken sandwiches tasted like blotting paper in his dry mouth and the pickles like sandpaper; found also, as his wrist watch ticked on, that his voice was gone, that his hands were cold and clammy, and that his stomach felt queer.

There remained only two hours until the race now. He said that he must hurry and change. Did she mind being left alone till he came back? He was assured that she did not. Taking his suitcase he went to the dressing room, and no sooner had he left than Roswell Schnell deserted his roadster for the vacant seat in Davis' Ford. Margie did not tell Roswell that she had discovered him before. She seemed surprised at the coincidence and so did he.

When Davis returned, radiant in white breeches, black top-boots and blue-and-white racing silks, he found them deeply engrossed in each other; but as soon as she saw him, Margie was all enthusiasm. She introduced the two men again, for neither offered to claim acquaintanceship.

Schnell helped himself to their lunch, look amused at Davis' costume, and after a while leisurely excused himself and wandered off.

"Do you like him?" said Davis blankly.

"Oh, I think he's amusing, don't you?"

Johnnie Walker arrived in a big horse-van and looked over the gathering crowd disdainfully. Alvin, who had followed the van in his own car, superintended the unloading, felt the bandaged legs and slapped the mahogany flanks with gruff affection. Then he came over and greeted the pair who were watching operations, greatly impressed.

He bowed ceremoniously to Margie and smiled knowingly at Davis.

"Well, Jock, feeling fit?"

Davis nodded, not daring to trust his voice. The horse was led into the paddock and the groom at his head walked him round and round.

"Let's be getting weighed, Jock."

Leaving Margie in charge of Schnell, who turned up opportunely, they went to the scales. Alvin gave him a saddle and lead pad. He stood on the scales while the clerk checked his name by a list.

"Two more pounds," said the official.

"Where's that sweater I told you to bring, Dave?"

Davis had forgotten it. Alvin swore and borrowed two more pieces of lead from a rider who had just come off the scales.

"Sorry about the sweater, Alvin," Davis said, and as they went to the paddock to saddle, he slipped his lady's favor into his breeches pocket.

"Don't worry about that now. Everything's O. K. How do you feel?"

"All right, I think."

They began saddling. He watched Alvin and the trainer pulling straps and adjusting buckles, testing everything three times over. While they were about it a bugle blew. When they had finished Alvin took Davis aside.

"Now, there's nothing to worry about. Win, lose or draw, it's all right with me. Just remember what I told you and keep your head. There are a couple of rough riders in the race. Watch out for them." (He pointed out two men.) "They'll do anything to win and you're on the favorite."

"I thought this race was for gentleman jockeys," said Davis, feebly.

"My boy, there are no gentleman jockeys, just as there are no lady whores."

Davis swallowed hard. Why did people call racing a sport? he wondered. It was more like a war.

There sounded another bugle.

"All up," called someone.

Alvin poured resin into his oozing hands and slapped him on the shoulder.

"All right, Dave., An iron cross or a wooden one, as we used to say in Flanders' fields."

Someone was hoisting him into the saddle, was adjusting more straps, was asking him if the stirrups were right. Johnnie Walker quivered, tossed his head and pawed the ground. There was a long line of horses being led through a lane of people. There was shouting. There was emptiness in his stomach and weakness in his arms.

They passed the betting row, and the bookmakers were calling:

"Last chance, men. Here's your prices. Two to one, Lochinvar; two to one, Earthquake; even money, Johnnie Walker; even money, Sinbad."

The groom let loose the horse's head and he bucked and plunged. Davis prayed that he would not fall off before the race began. A few moments more and they reached the starting flag. Here was great confusion. The starter swore at the riders, the riders swore back. One horse was kicking, another was rearing. Twice they were called back after a false start.

Davis felt himself being shuffled about like a child in a subway. The starter bellowed at him.

"Come on you, number six, cut the comedy. Turn that horse around."

Davis obeyed, but no sooner had he turned about than the flag dropped and the starter yelled, "Go!"

He had disregarded his first instructions, "Don't get left at the post." He had lost ten or twelve

lengths before he started. He was last at the first
fence.

Alvin's instructions had not covered this situation,
and Davis, chagrined and excited, wondered what to
do. But it soon proved that he had no choice. Johnnie
Walker was not pleased with the unfamiliar sight of
a dozen pairs of heels before him, and took it upon
himself to bring about a change.

He ran at the second fence as if it were thin air,
caught the top rail under his knees and threw it half-
way into the next field. Davis clutched at the mane
to stay on. He lost a stirrup and almost fell off over
the next fence. They were no longer last. Johnnie
Walker's blood was up. The farther he went the
faster he ran. He fairly elbowed his way through
a group of horses across the next field.

Davis thrilled with a new sensation. The glory
of speed, of danger, of competition; the smell of hot
flesh, and hot breath; the wind in his face, the blood
in his cheeks; the riding of a fast horse over green
grass. For a few minutes he could do nothing but
abandon himself to the compelling passion of the great
adventure.

Then his head cleared. They jumped into a plowed
field and he remembered that his orders were to cross
it slowly. For the first time in the race he opposed
his own judgment to the horse's and the horse yielded.
Clods of dirt flew back in his face and he shifted his
line to avoid them. Alvin's advice came back to him
easily now.

"Wait till you're through the plow and over the
ridge before you worry about getting to the front.
After you get over the thirteenth fence and hit that
down slope, give him his head. Get to the front as
soon as you can after that, and stay there."

Davis eased his horse up over the ridge. The

twelfth jump flashed beneath them. A bad turn and then the thirteenth.

Johnnie Walker was tiring. He had run faster than any horse in the race and he was carrying a green rider. He hit the thirteenth fence, went to his knees, and just managed to stand up.

Davis struggled back off the horse's neck into the saddle. One of his rivals was rolling on the ground a little to one side. This was the place to make his run. He called on the tiring animal as if he were advancing the throttle of his car.

Johnnie Walker had been doing his best all the race. Now he did better than his best. He chased the leaders down the slope, caught them at the bottom and pushed his steaming nostrils to the front as they jumped the next to last fence. There was a long up-grade now before the last fence and the stretch. Davis for the first time in his life experienced the thrill of leading the field. Victory, glory and romance waited for him at the finish.

But Johnny Walker had been badly ridden, his wind had been pumped by the clumsy seat of his rider, his mouth had been jabbed, his back and legs had been weakened. He was a weary horse as he breasted the last hill, which challenged the freshest and fittest after three miles of fast galloping. He got no encouragement from the lump of weight on his back. He had never been ridden like this before. Perhaps it wasn't a real race, perhaps it didn't matter. Johnnie Walker dropped his head and let his ears flop back.

There was a rush from behind, a creaking of leather, a heaving of tired breaths. Two horses passed an indolent little animal who was carrying a dead weight for a rider. They were up the hill. The last fence was before them.

But Johnnie Walker, lion-hearted son of Red Label, knew it was a race now. There was the cheering crowd, the home stretch and the winning post. He had seen them all before. There were two horses ahead of him and another coming up on his flank. Johnnie Walker called on his tired back and aching legs. His head came up, his ears pricked forward and, shouldering the load that was slipping about like a bag of oats, he started to run.

No horseman who saw the race ever said again that Johnnie Walker owed his success entirely to Alvin's skill. They never said he was too small or too frail. They admitted that any horse, after being left at the post, run into the ground, caught dead-heat four hundred yards from home—any horse that, after such a journey, could summon speed, strength and courage enough to catch and to beat Sinbad, Lochinvar and Earthquake—in short, they agree with Alvin that Johnnie Walker was not a great horse, but a super-horse.

As Davis came back to the judges' stand to weigh in and receive the cup, he was not thinking of the heroic little animal beneath him. He reached in his breeches pocket to feel the pasteboard and thought that here was the power and the glory. Here was the cheering, admiring crowd, here victory and here—ah, yes, there she was—his lady-love with worshipping eyes and waving handkerchief. Looking down, as Alvin led the winner into the paddock, he caught her eye and smiled a smile of conquest which she acknowledged, smiling back.

Davis and Margie stopped at the Madingly post office to telegraph the news home. Davis poised his pencil over the yellow sheet wondering how to word it. After a few seconds he wrote out a message and showed it to Margie saying:

"This is what Stonewall Jackson wired General Lee one afternoon."

She took it and read, "Providence blessed our arms with victory today."

XV

When Davis returned to Kingston University after the holiday he was struck by the incongruity of his position there. A champion of the rabble. Somehow he no longer felt the old enthusiasm for his cause. His triumphant visit at home had shown him that he was bred and trained for different things. It was one thing to be *for* the mob, quite another to be *of* it. Davis remembered the people who came to his father's house in Cranston and shuddered when he thought of those who came to his own room in Kingston. He did not want to be a snob. There was Christ, the Son of God Himself, who fraternized with fishermen and dined with publicans. The Bible and the Declaration of Independence both proclaimed the equality of men. Davis tried to believe it.

To the disgust of his southern colleagues, Davis joined the Lincoln Society, an anti-club organization composed entirely of non-club members. Here, too, he was an alien. He sat in the meetings huddled up in a corner with his clothes drawn about him as if to keep them from the common touch. He repulsed their gestures of familiarity, nodded to avoid shaking hands, and agreed with everything said rather than engage in an argument.

Yet, in spite of his lack of response, the society elected him, though a freshman, to its board of governors. It included the reform bill he had drawn up last term in its official file and gave him a rising vote of confidence and thanks for the courage he had displayed before the dean and the senior committee. It even asked him to make a memorial address for

107

their departed brother, Richard Damp, but he excused himself.

Davis had noticed before that people of the Damp type were very likely to be virtuous. Now he found also that they were almost invariably religious. The Christian Soldiers' Association had almost the same roll-call as the Lincoln Society. This group was organized with military grades; that is, there were generals, colonels, majors, captains and sergeants. There were no privates, strange to say, but this was explained in that the Association had taken it upon itself to lead the world to salvation.

One morning Davis received a postcard which requested Captain Pettigrier to be at headquarters Saturday at eight. He was completely mystified, until some half-hour later one of the most objectionable of his Lincoln acquaintances charged through the door and offered a spongy hand.

"Congratulations."

Davis pushed his own hand into his pocket and dried it on the cloth.

"Thanks," he said dryly. "What for?"

"Why, you've been made a captain right off. Most everyone has to serve as corporal and sergeant first, but they shoved you right up."

"It's very flattering, I'm sure, but I didn't even know I had enlisted. Did they do that for me, too?" He breathed a silent prayer of thanksgiving that Tom was out.

"Yes, oh, yes, don't worry, everything's been arranged."

Saturday night Davis declined Phil's invitation to go to the moving pictures. He reported at headquarters, which turned out to be the Sunday School room of the Baptist Church. He was greeted by his enthusiastic friend and presented to General Harper, who called him "Dave" and put his arm on his shoulders ninety seconds after the introduction.

General Harper called the meeting to order, by standing on the platform and shouting, "Ten-shun!" The General was a man of about thirty, strongly built, big-shouldered and rather handsome. He had graduated from Kingston eight years ago and left some reputation as an athlete behind him. He had gone to a seminary and now held the position of assistant pastor at the First Baptist Church. From the time of his taking office about two years ago, Harper had interested himself in the souls of the undergraduates and had organized the body of which he was now leader.

"We will begin as usual by a salute to our Commander-in-Chief."

Whereupon the General whirled about and, facing the wall where hung a picture of Christ, raised his right hand in military salute. Davis saw that all others in the room had assumed the same attitude and he quickly followed suit.

After the demonstration the General again addressed his troops, who were now seated.

"Soldiers, before we go any farther we must welcome to our ranks a newcomer, though I am sure not a stranger. He has won the right to be here through his gallant defense of a cause dear to us all. On behalf of the Christian Soldiers, Captain Pettigrier, I welcome you."

There was applause and Davis' neighbor nudged and whispered to him to get up. He rose. The applause redoubled, then suddenly subsided as if they expected a speech. Davis was dumb with embarrassment. He could think of nothing to say; so with the courage of despair he drew himself up to attention, gave the General a brisk salute and sat down.

"Now let us bow our heads in silent prayer and see

if we can get orders from our Commander. I might say for the benefit of any of our new soldiers that this association is run entirely by Divine guidance. We believe that if one gives God a chance to speak, He will, if He has any special wishes. It is through guidance that we brought Captain Pettigrier to our banner. Let us pray."

The room bowed its head and rested it on the palm of its hand. For fully five minutes there were only accidental sounds such as sneezes and shufflings. Then the General said, "Amen."

The man next to Davis, however, did not move, but remained in his devout position for another sixty seconds while the room waited on his leisure. Finally he straightened up and looked triumphantly about.

Harper indicated that the meeting was open to the house. Davis' neighbor stood up and was recognized.

"I had a hunch," he declared, laying a slight tap of emphasis on the slang word, as if to indicate that he was not above its use, "that I should tell how Christ came into my life, in hopes that it will do somebody some good."

Davis felt uncomfortably certain that this was addressed to him. By the expression of those about him he judged that they had heard these adventures before.

"When I first came to college three years ago I was a very different person from what I am now. I had different ideas and different values. I was frivolous, even wild. I smoked, I drank, and—yes, I confess, for the good it may do someone here—I swore. I was very much the kind we have so many of here at Kingston today, the kind who rush off to the city and —and misbehave. I know all the temptations; I had them once myself. Had them, did I say? Soldiers, I confess for your benefit that I still have them, but by the grace of my Leader I shall not sin again."

He paused, overcome by the thought of his own

struggles, and Davis took the opportunity of looking him over. He found it hard to reconcile the short, soft, bovine-countenanced individual that he saw with the picture of the rollicking young devil the individual was portraying himself to be. He found it difficult to imagine this person trooping off on a "bender" with Tom, Phil and Johnson. It was a ridiculous thought and he stifled it quickly.

"Yes, I led a life of sin until one day I met a man. I talked to the man and soon I confessed the story of my life. This man led me out of the muck and filth to Christ and salvation. Soldiers, that man was General Jake Harper!"

With this dramatic climax he sat down. Harper smirked modestly as the soldiers gave him a round of applause. Another man whom Davis could not see got up and gave an intimate account of his temptations and final victory through the grace of his Leader. Several more followed of more or less the same substance. It was so disgusting and unmanly that Davis wondered how they could make such exhibitions in public. What did this all have to do with religion, he asked himself again and again.

A greasy-looking soldier had the floor now and was saying there was a girl in town who needed their help. She was about to take the road to ruin; in fact, had started in that direction already. He asked the General for a detachment to rescue her. Davis gathered that he meant a committee to call and point out her errors to her. He imagined how Alvin would snort over this, and could not prevent a smile curling the corners of his own mouth.

The smile was petrified on his lips the next moment, however, when the General said that this was a chance for their newest member to win his spurs, and read out "Pettigrier" among a list of five. This committee was to convene after the main meeting was over.

"Good Lord!" thought Davis irreverently.

Captain Pettigrier made for the door as soon as General Harper had dismissed the formation. He deafened and blinded himself to all that might delay him. He slipped out of the door, walked brisky to the corner of the building, and then broke into a run that carried him swiftly to the shelter of his room.

"Hello, Dave, been to the show?" asked Tom as he burst in.

"Yes, funniest thing I ever saw. Didn't know whether to laugh or cry."

"I didn't see anything funny about it, especially when he gets shot for desertion."

"I didn't wait to see whether he got shot or not," Davis confessed.

This fiasco caused Davis to make up his mind definitely. He was very positive now where he belonged. It was absurd to continue his intimacy with that crowd of riff-raff, he thought. He could never understand them nor they him. His loyalty forbade a sudden severance of all relations, but he was determined to break quietly and gradually with the Lincoln Society and the Christian Soldiers. Perhaps he would keep his membership in the society. It had its good points and, besides, it would seem caddish to be too pointed in the matter. He would not hurt anyone's feelings if he could help it. But, one way or another, to break off from this whole group he was determined.

Besides this he must reclaim his rightful place in college. He would go with Tom's friends, force himself to like them, and them to like him. He would make no public renunciation of his ultimatum on the club system, but would let it be understood that he had resumed a less belligerent attitude. He was sure it would all die a natural death, be buried and forgotten. Next year he would join the Owl Club and live as befitted his birth and breeding.

Accordingly he set about to make these changes. When one of the soldiers called to summon him to a meeting of the sub-committee on virtue, Davis thanked him, promised to try and be there, but did not go. He cut the Lincoln Society meetings and ignored a postcard commanding Captain Pettigrier to report at headquarters for a lecture by some well-known evangelist.

Pride made him hesitant in his advances to the other set. Johnson he distinctly disliked and the others he hardly knew. By keeping Tom in sight he managed to be in their company, but they never warmed to him or accepted him except as "Stevenson's roommate."

One evening well into the third quarter of the term, Tom got up from the desk where he had been working and straddled the empty fireplace. It was plain that something was resting heavily on his mind.

"Dave, I've been thinking—"

"Go on," chaffed Davis, "tell me another."

"Well, I mean it's pretty plain that things are funny, isn't it?"

"Some things, I admit, are funny. You aren't insinuating that I am, are you?"

"Well, now, Dave, let's be frank. You've got your friends and I've got mine. You don't like mine and I'm not crazy about yours. What I was thinking was that we might as well admit it."

Davis was silent. He thought he knew what was coming, but dared not assume it yet.

"We got a notice this morning, Dave. Did you see it?"

He took an envelope off the mantelpiece and tossed it to his friend. Davis had seen it. It was an application for rooms next year. It was to be filled out and returned if they intended to keep their present ones.

"Well," he said.

Tom looked everywhere but toward Davis and tried to go on. Davis interrupted.

"I understand, Tom. You've forgotten the lines Johnson taught you. You want to say that next year you and he will room together here and I must get out."

"Oh, no, Dave, not like that."

Davis rose, went quietly into his bedroom and shut the door without turning on the light. So Tom was leaving him. An army of memories marched through his brain. Tom leaving! Quarrels they had had a plenty. What friends had not? But to separate! They who had been unsworn comrades-in-arms since days forgot. The fun they had together, the places they had been, the times they had talked. Tom, the word. It was tied up with his childhood, boyhood, youth, happiness, home—with Margie. And Tom was leaving, leaving because their friendship and affection had left long ago. He lay down gently on the bed and sobbed.

XVI

Jackson Pettigrier, new president of the Dial Engineering Company, watched the office door close on John Lucas before he returned to his seat behind the desk. He picked up a pencil and drew three triangles on the blotter. Then he joined the corners of triangles and made an irregular figure. He contemplated it gravely for a few minutes before he repeated the process.

So John Lucas wanted a loan, wanted it badly, or else he would have gone to a bank and borrowed it on securities. The fact that he had come to a man's office and begged for a private loan might indicate that he had no securities. Yet a few years ago Lucas had come to Cranston a rich man and head of a rich corporation.

Mr. Pettigrier was a shrewd man of business. People said he had made the Dial Company, when he was manager and vice-president. Now he was president and they congratulated him, saying: "I knew it all along. It was only a question of time."

He had seen enough of business to know what to take and what to leave alone. John Lucas' proposition was absurd on the face of it, Lucas ought to have seen that himself. Yet Mr. Pettigrier had not pointed out the absurdity to his visitor. On the other hand he had heard him through without an interruption and politely agreed to consider the matter.

Jackson Pettigrier had given his life to an ideal. His youth that had faded so quickly had not been bartered for the privilege of sitting behind a door with "President" painted on the outside, nor for a house in the country, nor for anything else he could see or touch. Those nights in sleeping cars, those days away from home, they were all in open exchange for what the practical business man had coveted for over twenty years. That expensive, coveted thing was something as intangible as a father's love and pride.

Yet in spite of a quarter of a century's labor, he had not relaized his dearest wish. He knew that his son was neither happy nor successful. He knew that when Davis returned to college within the next few days he did so with loathing and distaste. Mr. Pettigrier was a discerning man. There was no need to ask his son why he had broken with his roommate last spring, or why he did not bring home friends from college as others did. What the father had not guessed Alvin Martin had supplied. Mr. Pettigrier knew that his son was a social outcast at college and was not so because of vice, but of virtue. He knew that Davis was lonely, bitter and unhappy because he was too good.

He hardly knew whether he and his wife were to blame or not. All parents tried to teach their children to stand straight by telling them to lean over backwards, thus allowing for the bias of original sin. The failures of the system were usually to the other extreme, and parents whose children manage to walk with any semblance of perpendicularity were to be congratulated. But here was the one example in ten million where the child had actually retained the shape in which he was molded.

Probably some day the world would iron him out straight, but it would be a painful process and there was always the chance of cracking the substance which time makes brittle.

Mr. Pettigrier could not blame himself for this freak of nature. If he had it to do again he knew he would do almost the same. The question was now how to make the best of a bad situation. That was why he did not give John Lucas a flat refusal.

It would take much less than a father's eye to see the condition of Davis' heart and a memory much less keen than Jackson Pettigrier's to forget his own young love. If there was anything to bring an unquiet, worried mind to rest, he thought, it was a loving wife and a happy home. Therefore, when John Lucas came to him in difficulty Mr. Pettigrier drew triangles on his blotter and was thoughtful.

He arose, put on his hat and crossed the street to the office of Alvin Martin, attorney at law. The barrister seemed a little surprised to see a man with whom he had lunched an hour ago.

"Business call, Alvin; we presidents don't often make them, you know."

"Don't blame you. You've made your share of business calls. Don't suppose you'll do much now you're boss."

"Not a bit more than I can help, I'll tell you. I want to stay home with the family for the next twenty-five years. Doesn't do to leave a pretty wife alone too much."

"So they say," rejoined his friend.

"Now to get down to business. Alvin, Lucas came around just now—wanted to borrow some money. Says his daughter's a debutante this year and he needs a little to see him through the season, what with the parties, dresses and all."

"Did you ask him why he didn't go to a bank?"

"Didn't have to; he told me he didn't happen to have any securities in hand that he could use. I put him off and thought that if you could tell me something that wasn't confidential about Grafton Chemicals—"

"I know plenty about Grafton Chemicals, all right,

Jackson, and you will, too, before long, but there isn't much I'm at liberty to tell."

"Suppose Lucas met you in the club tonight and asked for a loan of, say, ten thousand dollars for six months, what would you say?"

"I'd say, 'Now I'll tell one.' I'm not speaking as attorney for Grafton Chemicals now. I'm only telling you as a friend, don't cast your bread on the waters, it looks like rain."

"Still, poor chap, he wants to give his daughter a good time. She's a nice child, too."

"If you are looking for a charity to endow I suggest the Red Cross, but as a matter of business—hands off."

"All right, Alvin, thanks a lot. Good-bye."

He recrossed the street and returned to his own desk. Ten thousand dollars. He had that in round numbers put aside to take Molly and Davis to Europe this summer. If Lucas repaid it in six months he would never miss it. But then Alvin ought to know. Mr. Pettigrier drew some more triangles. Things in this world are only worth what you're willing to give for them, he mused. If he could help Lucas out of a tight place, Lucas would be very glad to do him a favor some day. Of course, he told himself, he was the last person in the world to bargain in affairs such as this, but after all there was such a thing as diplomacy. He remembered how much easier his winning of Molly Davis had been because her parents had favored him. Molly had never been coerced, he was sure, but everything helped in these matters.

Suppose, for instance, Grafton Chemicals should fail. Lucas would certainly want his daughter to marry where she would not need his help. There were dozens of legitimate ways in which parents could influence a daughter's choice.

Naturally he would not think of mentioning this

to Lucas. That would be too indelicate. It was not as if he were loaning money with the idea of compensation. The way matters stood, a refusal would be doing something that might possibly hurt his son's happiness, and Mr. Pettigrier wanted to think twice before doing it. If ten thousand dollars could have purchased Davis' happiness outright, he would have considered it cheaply bought.

Besides, Mr. Pettigrier continued to try to justify himself for thinking such thoughts, no gentleman would borrow money unless he had good reason to know he could repay it. And John Lucas was a gentleman. He would lend Lucas the money as a friend and neighbor. At any rate he would think it over.

XVII

When Davis returned to Kingston in the fall he found that in the spring drawing he had been allotted the room that Richard Damp had had the year before. He immediately set about to exchange his room for another in a more congenial community. However, all the rooms were officially assigned, and his only chance was to find someone willing to trade. This he was unable to do immediately, and after two weeks of fruitless effort he ceased trying. He made it a point to have as little as possible to do with his neighbors, Tom Stevenson and Bob Johnson.

The first term passed without open hostilities. Tom tried clumsily to resume some sort of friendly relations, but was sternly rebuffed. The second term opened on the club election activities and they avoided each other carefully.

Davis did not continue his anti-club campaign. He dropped all connection with the Lincoln Society and the Christian Soldiers. He stood mailed in his own pride and defiance between two contesting armies, a belligerent neutral to both.

He had foreseen this situation when he separated from Tom, but had not realized what it would really be. The loneliness was inconceivable. Last year he had been opposed, derided and a little admired; now he was ignored, neglected. No club would have dared to show him any attention, nor any sophomore to become identified as his friend. He ate alone, walked alone, lived alone. Stoically he applied himself to his work, and his work prospered. His masters praised him. Davis did not want their praise, did

not relish it. He worked because he could not play.
His one solace was Margie. She wrote regularly
from Cranston, where she was making her début.
Glowing, radiant letters they were, with the fragrance
of flowers and the gaiety of dance music. He had
seen her at Christmas and she was the same as ever,
joyous, lovely and happy. He had asked her just
before he left to come to the February prom, but she
had been forced to decline, for Tom had invited her.
Davis had been angry only with himself. He should
have asked her sooner. Without saying so, she gave
him to understand that she wished he had.

The date of the prom came. He had said he would
not go to the dance, but a letter that morning caused
him to change his mind. At ten o'clock that evening
he started to dress. An hour later he entered the
gymnasium.

There she was, prim and pretty, clad like a descended
angel all in white. He danced with her and she glided
in his arms like a "disembodied joy." He forgot all
his troubles, overlooked the snubbings of people who
knew him, and reveled silently in an unfamiliar happiness. For nobody else, it seemed, did she wear that
smile or that shining light in her eyes. Nobody else
did she move so trustingly close to when she danced.
He knew it as surely as he knew he breathed. She
loved him, as surely as he loved her.

Davis hardly noticed the hours as they glided by
to the rhythm of the orchestra. It was supper time
before he realized it, and he had not asked her to sit
out. After supper he would. He saw her go up on
the balcony with Tom. He moved so as to watch
her unobserved.

Tom brought her chicken salad, and she ate it dain-
tily, then ice cream, then coffee. Now she leaned over
the railing and seemed listless. How carelessly she

handled her own lovely body, how little she seemed to appreciate the privilege of living within it.

He thought of the balcony scene in *Romeo and Juliet*. No Romeo ever looked on a lady such as this. Almost unconsciously he quoted to himself:

"See how she leans her cheek upon her hand.
O, that I were a glove upon that hand,
That I might touch that cheek."

Supper was over. He cut in quickly and asked his boon. She smiled and nodded as if to say, "It's time you did ask."

He chose a car at approximately the same spot where they had sat last year.

"Oh, Margie, I want to tell you something. I love you. I want to exaggerate it, but I can't even get within shouting distance of the way I feel."

"Davis, don't. I'm so upset. I'm in a terrible mess. What shall I do?"

"What is it, Margie? Tell me."

Her serious mood quelled his ardor for a moment and he asked again, more quietly this time.

"What is it?"

"Well, first, will you not be shocked if I show you something?"

"No," he promised, puzzled.

She took a small box from her vanity case and extracted a cigarette.

"I started to smoke this year. Do you mind?"

It was a jolt to his illusions, seeing an angel smoke, but he tried not to show it and said bravely:

"Of course not."

She lit the cigarette and used it with tell-tale ease.

"Was that all that bothered you?" he asked.

"Oh, no, Davis. It's worse, much worse. Promise not to tell."

He promised.

"Well, it all started when you didn't invite me soon enough, and I accepted Tom."

"Accepted him—"

"Oh, no, not that way. Accepted his invitation. When he came to get me tonight he had a car. We drove down by the lake and I noticed that he'd been drinking terribly. He stopped the car and when I asked him to go on, he wouldn't. Then, Davis, he tried to kiss me."

"God Almighty."

"Now, Davis, don't get so excited; I wouldn't let him."

"I'll kill him, I swear to God I'll kill him."

"Davis, Davis, you promised you wouldn't tell a soul."

"I won't tell, Margie, but I'm going to get him for it. You'll see."

"Oh, why did I ever tell you? I knew I shouldn't. Listen, Davis, he wasn't himself, he was drunk as could be. There's nothing to get so excited about. People have tried before."

"I don't care," he raged. "Tom of all people."

"Davis, if you want to do something for me, do it now—and forget I ever told you. Please, Davis, please."

She took him by the shoulders and made him face her. He quivered at her touch. He could feel the warm glow from her hands on his neck and cheeks.

She tried again and again to make him promise, but he would not. She sobbed gently and said, "Oh, my God!" which shocked him still more.

He was oblivious to her charms now, and as long as they sat he only answered her gruffly behind his teeth. Finally they went in. He felt her hand linger pleadingly on his shoulder when he was broken, and he knew she was watching when he left the room.

Down in the basement of the gymnasium were the locker rooms, where the students dressed for athletics in season. Now they were used for quite a different purpose. It was here that the male dancers descended to refresh themselves with alcohol. In corners and behind rows of lockers huddled groups of guilty young men with bent elbows and tilted chins.

Here it was that Davis sought Tom. Twice he walked through the aisles looking into nooks and alcoves. Baffled, he turned to go elsewhere, but suddenly remembered that one place he had forgotten, the squash court.

He went into a passage and up a few steps. There was a light in the court and as he approached he heard voices. The door was half open. He pushed his way in. There were half a dozen young bloods well on the way to drunkenness—and one of them was Tom Stevenson.

Davis shouldered two astonished young men aside and leaped at his enemy. Someone seized him from behind, but, spinning, Davis shook him off, cast a fist in the general direction and returned to his original foe.

Tom had been caught unawares, but now he was ready. He met the mad rush with a right-handed swing that sent Davis reeling. Again there was intervention. This time Davis escaped his captor in time to reach Tom's unprotected face with a hard smash. Tom's arms were pinioned to his sides and he was unable either to escape the blow or to return it. Stung to a supreme effort, he freed himself and they met in a headlong rush that staggered them both.

A crowd had been attracted by the noise and was pushing through the small door. Some were trying to separate the fighters, others were shouting to let them alone. Suddenly out of the unintelligible chaos rose one sound that quieted all, as if a magic spell had been cast over the scene.

"Proctors!   Proctors!"

Two burly dreadnaughts plowed through the seething maelstrom that centered about the object of interest.   In less than a minute peace was restored and the small room cleared of all except the principals.

"You'll be telling your troubles to the dean, never mind anything but your names now," said a thick Irish brogue.

Davis was escorted back to his room under a double guard, and Tom, who pleaded that he had a partner, was permitted to remain at the dance.   Before Davis had a chance to sit down and think over the situation Phil Parsons came in and took charge of things immediately.

"Go down and take a shower, Dave.   Wash the blood off your face and when you've cooled down a bit come back.   I want to talk to you, if you don't mind."

Davis obeyed meekly and returned in a few minutes refreshed and considerably calmer.   In spite of the hour—it was past four—he was not sleepy and rather glad Phil had come.

"Dave, you've made a nice mess of things, haven't you?   You'll probably get a suspension, but if it's cured you of some of your bad habits I'll say it's worth it."

Davis flared up again.   "What bad habits?   I hadn't had a drink."

"Do you want me to tell you something for your own good, or would you rather find it out some other way?"

"I don't know what you're talking about."

"All right, I'll tell you, but don't start another fight with me.   If you do, I'll just walk out.   Now, in the first place, I know without being told what it was all about. I've been expecting it for a long time. It was over that girl, wasn't it?"

"None of your business."

"I thought so. You found out something about her that you wouldn't believe, didn't you? Now, Dave, listen. For three or four years you've been blind. You've refused to use your eyes because you didn't want to know certain facts. Tonight you found out Margie's been kissed and you ran wild."

"That's a damn lie!" Davis leaped out of his chair. "She never has."

"Yes, she has, Dave, honest. You might as well know it. That girl has been kissed to my certain knowledge by at least a dozen persons, including myself."

Now the truth was out. The truth he had always shunned, dreaded, refused to hear, had been shouted at him. He sat down again quietly.

"I'm mighty sorry, Dave, but it's true. I'm only telling you for your own good. You couldn't go on after this without knowing. But it doesn't mean a thing. All girls have. If they hadn't they wouldn't be worth knowing."

Davis sat dumbly. Phil tried several times to get him to speak, but failed.

"I'll be going, then, Dave. Good-night."

"Good-night, Phil."

XVIII

Bundled to his ears in a heavy overcoat, Alvin
Martin plunged out of the City Club into the snow.
It was one of those sifting, indolent snows that are
typical of the near-South. Before morning it would
cease, and by noon the woolly carpet would melt into
slush. A few flakes slipped in between the brim of
his hat and the upturned collar of his coat. They
settled pleasantly on his nose and lips.

He looked forward to a quiet evening alone among
his books. It had been a hard day at the office, turning over page after page, looking up precedents that
might help him on this Lucas case. It looked hopeless, he thought, but he liked hopeless cases. He had
won them before. He would go over and over this
data till he found a loophole, some legal quibble that
would unsettle the jury and save John Lucas a visit
to prison.

Not that he had any personal sympathy for his
client. Nothing was too bad for a man who employed
fraud against the government in time of war. Why,
it was almost treason. Some of the Liberty Bond
money, that patriots gave to help the cause, had gone
into Lucas' pocket.

It would all be in the papers soon. They made so
much of things like that. He remembered a lawyer
in Washington telling him that the scandal of the
century would be in print within a few months. Something about oil out West, "Teapot Dome," the man
had said over and over. "Wait till the papers get
that catch-phrase."

Alvin was glad the day was over. He had really

127

intended to spend the evening at the club, but some-how he enjoyed men's company less every day.

"There's nothing like a good book, unless it's a fast horse," he mumbled, fishing in an inside pocket for his key-ring.

He ran up the narrow stairs in his eagerness to settle down, selecting another key for the door at the top of the steps.

"Confound that black scoundrel, he's left the light on again."

He threw his overcoat on a chair and his hat and gloves on top of it. Then for the first time he noticed he was not alone.

"Tommie, what in God's name—"

"Hush, Alvin, don't talk like that. If you want to know why I'm here I'll tell you without being sworn at. He has gone north suddenly, to Kingston. The prodigal son's in trouble again."

"In trouble? What's he done?"

"Oh, I don't know. In some sort of drunken brawl."

"Nothing in the world would do that boy more good than a few drunken brawls. He's too damn virtuous."

"Like his mother, I suppose you mean."

"His mother's all right."

"You used to think she was more than all right, Alvin. I suppose I shouldn't have come tonight, I don't seem very welcome."

He came to her and took her hands. "I'm sorry, Tommie, if I seem gruff. I've had a hellish day down town. This Grafton Chemical business is a tough nut to crack."

"What's it all about, Alvin? Will they put John Lucas in jail?"

"Maybe. You wouldn't understand it, even if I explained. It's over a war contract, that's all. The only thing I'm sure of is that Grafton Chemicals is going on the rocks in a hurry."

"That kind of thing never interests me." She got up and went to the window, pulling aside the curtain.

"Alvin, when you realize that every single snowflake is entirely different and so is every man, animal and fish in the world—doesn't it make you believe in God? No man can approach the works of God."

"I don't know about that, Tommie. Don't you see that it would be much harder to make all snowflakes the same than just to let them happen to be different? The Colgate Company turns out I don't know how many packages of tooth paste a day, every one the same. That's much more of a feat, I think."

"Is that why you're such a smart lawyer, Alvin, because nobody can ever get the last word?"

"Please don't stand there in front of the window. Anyone can see you from the street."

She flounced back to the sofa. "Are you ashamed of me?"

He neither answered nor moved.

"I asked you a question, Alvin." Her voice was a trifle petulant.

"Ashamed of you? No, of course not. You're not mine to be either proud or ashamed of. You're another man's wife. Better ask him."

"I think I'd better go. You're not in the best of humors tonight."

"Don't go, Tommie," he said, although she had made no attempt to do so. "I'm a little tired, that's all."

He went to a cupboard, poured himself a whiskey and soda and returned to her side on the sofa. They both seemed ill at ease. He made an attempt to break

"I'm going to write a book. These are the notes the barriers of self-consciousness.
I've taken."

"What about, Alvin?"

"Oh, life and love and fate, I reckon. That's all I know anything about."

"Don't tell me you're going to write one of those indecent modern novels. I think they're disgusting. How can they write such trash? It used to be that people wouldn't stand for it, but nowadays they revel in it. It'll be the ruination of the young. Why, Alvin, you don't realize how wicked these children are. And it's mostly because they see things in print that we didn't even dare to think when we were young. The Lord only knows what they'll grow up to be, without any reticence or respect for anything."

"I don't think my book will corrupt anyone. I doubt if anyone ever reads it. There're so many good books around."

"All modern literature is bad and indecent."

Alvin was unable to check his characteristic snort at this, but he softened it with an affectionate chuckle.

"If you laugh, it just shows you don't know modern literature. You haven't read anything but your old poets that are dead and gone."

"You're right," Alvin had to admit, "I've read too much old poetry."

Suddenly he threw back his head and laughed with spontaneous abandon.

"What's so funny? I don't think it's very polite to roar in my face like that. I think you've had enough to drink. Give me that."

Alvin drank the remainder of the liquid and handed her the glass.

"I've got some news that will sober you up, only promise if I tell you, you won't threaten to go to Mexico and start a revolution."

"Go on, Tommie. Tell me."

"My brother came in just as I was leaving tonight. I said I was sorry but I was going slumming. He said that reminded him he had something to tell me. 'If I were you,' he said, 'I'd let up on this slumming, now your husband is going to be home a lot.' He looked so wise that I asked him a few questions and finally he said he knew all about us; that is, about you and me."

Alvin said, "My God!" but did not stir.

"He said he had known it for almost five years, ever since you came back from France. He said that people in town were talking.

"My God!" said Alvin again, and this time he rose and walked to the window, gripping the curtain with white knuckles.

"Isn't it funny how we thought nobody knew?" she said.

"Funny! Yes, it's a perfect scream, isn't it? Go on, tell me, does *he* know?"

"Of course not. He wouldn't believe it if I told him. There's nothing to worry about."

"Worry about! Tommie, how can you sit there as if we were discussing the weather?"

"Alvin, I tell you there's no danger. Do you suppose Louis will say anything after he's known it for five years? He isn't so holy himself that he can throw stones."

"Well, of course I don't pretend to understand women, but all this is beyond me. You think it's funny and say there's nothing to worry about. Now, listen. This is the last straw. I was going to tell you soon anyhow. You're never to come here again. If you do, I shall have to leave. Do you think I can go to a man's house, sit at his table, call him my friend and know that the whole town is laughing at the farce? No, and by God I won't! For ten years I have, and it's time I stopped."

"But, Alvin, why is it any worse now than ten years ago?"

"It gets worse every day. Then we were younger and youth wás some excuse. Now we have no excuse at all. I mean it this time, Tommie. I never wanted this arrangement. You forced yourself on me, and because I loved you I let you make of me what you have. You must never enter this room again as long as you live."

"I see, you don't love me any more. You never did. You just used my love for your pleasure, and now you're finished with me and you throw me away." She burst into violent, hysterical sobs.

Alvin went to the cupboard and tossed three cubic inches of whiskey down his throat. He had seen ignorant, coarse women cry like that, but never a lady.

"You've got another woman to bring up here. That's why you don't want me."

"Now, Tommie, control yourself. Think what you're saying."

She sobbed and maligned him for another quarter of an hour, and he stood where he was offering neither consolation nor protest. Finally she rose and, picking up her wraps, went majestically to the door. Her pride seemed to have been restored. She scorned his attempt to help her on with her coat. As she seized the door knob, Alvin had laid his hand on hers.

"Tommie, don't go off like that. Can't you, won't you understand? I do love you. I wish to God I didn't, but I do. You must see my situation. There are things in a man's—a gentleman's—life that he has to put before his love."

She looked him fiercely in the eyes. "When a man puts other things before love, then he's ceased to love. If I don't mind what people say, why should you; you who hold people's opinions in such contempt?"

"I can't go into that again, Tommie. We can go on being friends as openly as you like, but no more

of this hiding up in a garret.   That part's all over,
Tommie."

She tugged at the door, but he resisted her.   "Tommie, may I kiss you good-bye?" he said, simply, almost bashfully.

Tossing her head, she replied, "Certainly not. What
would people say?"

He moved from the door and watched it close on
her back before walking to the cupboard and pouring
another drink.

XIX

Cleanliness being next to godliness people must hang
out their washing for the sun to dry on the day after
they have gone to church; and if the heavenly chari-
oteer has any consideration at all he will swoop down
near the earth on Monday mornings. The tenement
house dwellers of New York City were grateful for
this consideration on the first Monday of March, 1923.
So were the negro laundresses of Cranston, but Davis
Pettigrier, in Kingston, did not care. He felt the
warm flush on his cheek and on the back of the hand
that supported his chin, but he was not particularly
thankful. This day a year ago he had sat in the
window-seat of the room across the hall and watched
the scene in the courtyard with relative indifference.
As a flock of seagulls follow the wake of an ocean
liner, so did the crowd of sophomores trail the patient
postman around his beat. Last year, thought Davis,
another man sat where I sit, and now he sits no more.
Perhaps he thinks as men above the grass think, perhaps he cannot keep from thinking, he has so little else
to do.

Davis heard the outer door to his own entry open;
he heard the postman swing his bag down to the
floor, heard him whistling a ragtime tune as he sorted
the mail, heard the door across the hall open and
Tom's jubilant cheer as he received the envelope he
wanted. Davis had hoped beyond hope that he himself would receive a club invitation. Why he dared
to hope, he did not ask, for there was no answer.
He made himself wait till the letter-slot flipped open
and shut and two envelopes dropped through. Then
breathlessly he crossed the room and picked them up.

134

One, he knew at a glance was from Margie. The other was postmarked Kingston and was plain. It was the kind that clubs sent out with invitations. Perhaps his father's influence had forced the Owl Club to send him one. With clumsy fingers he opened it and with unseeing eyes tried to read the contents. It was fully thirty seconds before he comprehended its meaning.

> "For conduct unbecoming an officer and a Christian Soldier, we are forced hereby to suspend indefinitely your commission."

Davis caught his breath sharply as he allowed the sheet to glide off the palm of his hand to the rug. "Even the rats are deserting the sinking ship," he said coldly, and returned to the window seat with the other letter. Somehow he had let himself hope, allowed himself to wait for this morning's mail with expectation. But the inevitable had happened again as it always seemed to do in unpleasant matters. Up to today he had belonged at least nominally to the group from which the clubs would choose their new members. After today he belonged to one which they had turned down. Now he would be officially a derelict, an outcast, an undesirable. A Pettigrier belonged to the Great Unwanted. The sun, with unofficial, unjudging indifference, warmed his cheek and the back of his hand.

And Margie had written. It was almost two weeks now since the prom. In that time he had gone through many stages. At first he had sworn that since she had deceived him, had pretended to be what she was not, had made him love a personality and character that was not hers—at first he had sworn he hated her. Then came wave after wave of reaction; beating, surging, foaming against his wall of standards. He hated her, loved her, despised her; hated her, loved her, loved her, loved her. Now she had written, written, of course, to tell him she was sorry, to ask him to forgive, to say she admired him, thought he was wonderful, loved him.

There it was, the sweet, careless wiggle that she used for her d's, as when she wrote "Dear Davis." He let his eyes linger affectionately on the first two words. How he longed to hear her say them, she who wrote them with such white and careless fingers.

> "Dear Davis:
> "What do you think? Father and Mother are going to announce my engagement next Friday to Roswell Schnell. I wanted you to be the first to know. I am so happy and terribly in love and he has been perfectly wonderful to me this season. We are to be married on May 10th and you must be there to kiss the bride. Love.
> "Margie"

At about four-thirty in the afternoon of May tenth the sun cast some of its rays through the panes of a closed window. The rays passed undimmed through the glass, but some three inches beyond the glass they were almost dissipated in the drawn curtain. Beyond the curtain was a lighted room. Under a droplight in the centre stood a table and on the table sprawled the head and arms of a young man. The man's body rested in a sitting position on a chair.

Fourteen months ago under the same droplight had sprawled another young man. Richard Damp had only killed himself here, but Davis Pettigrier was torturing himself. He raised his head and sat up straight in the chair. On the table until now hidden by his arms and head lay an aged-frayed book. On a fly leaf was written: "To, Louis Davis Pettigrier from his mother on the day of his confirmation." It was an English prayer book that had belonged to his mother's grandmother.

Davis turned the pages until about the middle of the book he found the heading, "Solemnization of Matrimony." Modulating his voice to an audible whisper, he read:

"Dearly beloved, we are gathered together here in the sight of God and in the face of this company to join together this man and woman in Holy Matrimony; which is an honorable estate, instituted of God in the time of man's innocency, signifying unto us the mystic union that is between Christ and His Church; which holy estate Christ adorned and beautified with his presence, and first miracle that he wrought, in Cana of Galilee; and is commended of St. Paul to be honorable among all men; and therefore is not by any to be enterprised, nor taken in hand, unadvisedly, lightly or wantonly, to satisfy carnal lusts or appetites, like brute beasts that have no understanding; but reverently, discreetly, advisedly, soberly, and in the fear of God, duly considering the causes for which Matrimony was ordained.

"First, it was ordained for the procreation of children, to be brought up in the fear and nurture of the Lord, to be the praise of his holy name.

"Secondly, it was ordained for a remedy against sin, and to avoid fornication; that such persons that have not the gift of continency might marry and keep themselves undefiled members of Christ's body.

"Thirdly, it was ordained for the mutual society, help and comfort that one ought to have of the other, both in prosperity and adversity.

"Into which holy estate these two persons present come now to be joined. Therefore, if any man can show any just cause why they may not lawfully be joined together, let him now speak or else hereafter forever hold his peace."

Davis had been resting his cheek-bones against the knuckles of his hands while he read. Now he paused, looked up and rested his chin against his knuckles."

"Not one word about love," he thought, and, resuming his former position, continued to read.

"I require and charge you both, as ye will answer at the dreadful day of judgment when the secrets of hearts shall be disclosed, that if either of ye know any impediment, why ye may not be lawfully joined together in matrimony, ye do now confess it. For be ye well assured that so many as ye are coupled together otherwise than God's word doth allow are not joined together by God; neither is their Matrimony lawful.

"Wilt thou have this woman to be thy wedded wife, to live together after God's ordinance in the holy estate of Matrimony. Wilt thou love her, comfort her, honour and keep her in sickness and in health, and, forsaking all others, keep thee only unto her so long as ye both shall live?"

"I will."

"Wilt thou take this man to be thy wedded husband, to live together after God's ordinance in the holy estate of Matrimony? Wilt thou obey him and serve him, love, honor and keep him in sickness and in health, and, forsaking all others, keep thee only unto him, so long as ye both shall live?"

"I will."

"Who giveth this woman to be married to this man?"

Davis all but saw John Lucas three hundred miles distant give away his daughter. He all but heard Dr. Peckam cause Roswell to take Marjorie Lucas by the hand and repeat after him:

"I, Roswell, take thee, Marjorie, to be my wedded wife, to have and to hold from this day forward, for better, for worse, for richer, for poorer, in sickness and in health, to love and cherish, till death do us part, according to God's holy ordinance and therefore I plight my troth."

And then he heard Margie plight hers to Roswell Schnell.

"With this ring I thee wed, with my body I thee worship, and with all my worldly goods I thee endow. In the name of the Father, the Son and the Holy Ghost."

Davis closed the book. Margie Lucas was no more and a Mrs. Schnell lived in her lovely body.

In the two months that came between Margie's betrothal and her marriage, Davis Pettigrier had sat many times on his window-seat and thought: Why had she done such a thing? How could she, loving another man, allow him, Davis, to make love to her, and to hope? That always brought up the question, was she in love with Schnell? It seemed so incongruous to him. Margie, whom he had worshipped all these years as a goddess and adored as an angel, even when the veil of illusion had been rent, was still the Margie he loved as a woman. And even as the woman, allowing she was neither angel nor goddess, how could she love Roswell Schnell?

But if she were not in love, why did she marry? He remembered an evening, now five years ago, when he and Phil had argued. "People only marry for two things," Phil had said, "money and sex." Much as he hated to allow the possibility of this solution, Davis had considered it, but it gave no plausible answer. Mr. Lucas was a rich man, Margie an only child. There could be no pecuniary attraction in Schnell, and surely, surely he had little to offer in a physical way. Fat and thirty; slovenly, stupid and crude. That was how Davis, the jilted lover, described him, and an unbiased person could have been hardly more flattering.

Davis Pettigrier was not a conceited young man. He was proud of his ancestry and jealous of his name only because he had inherited it. He saw himself quite plainly now as a misunderstood, inefficient idealist, a failure. He did not consider himself worthy of Margie, because he did not consider that anybody was that. Yet deep in his heart he knew himself to be more so than Schnell. That was why the wound festered and pained. To be beaten by a better man, that was bad enough; but by one whom he had never deigned to consider a rival, was torment. To be disillusioned, jilted, defeated—it was all torment, but that was not the worst. What Davis dreaded most was to have to be alive and capable of thought on that night which was to be her bridal night. To think of those holy lips he had never touched being kissed by Schnell, and that sacred, lovely body he had been ashamed to notice, fondled and pawed.

Davis, like all men under stress, lacked this day a sense of proportion. Not only had he given vent to his feelings by reproducing the ceremony put on by the Holy Church, but he had determined to follow the action off stage to its ultimate and bitterest conclusion.

That is why he issued from his room this night about ten o'clock. Perhaps, too, it explained the wildness of his eye, the nervous strength of his stride and the rigidity of his carriage as he walked down Varsity Avenue, steering an undeviating course through the crowd of undergraduates returning from the picture show. He passed the Baptist church and noticed a light from the back window. The Christian soldiers were confessing their unsinned sins, he thought. Farther down the street was the Owl Club, with shadows of billiard players moving behind drawn curtains.

Turning definitely off Varsity Avenue, he plunged into Eden street, the underworld of the town folk, forbidden to students. A drunken negro lurched against him and Davis repulsively gave ground. His destination was Eden Hall, a place known to him only by reputation, and for its reputation he sought it out.

He found it, entered unaccosted but scrutinized and, leaning desperate elbows on the bar, called for a drink. It was vile stuff and he coughed over it. A silken shoulder brushed his and a rasping voice said, "Hello, dearie!"

He followed the woman upstairs to a small room lighted by a gas jet. It was murky, dense and smelt of uncleanliness. The woman lighted a cigarette by the gas and touched his arm. He shrank from her and went to the window.

There was a monochromatic view of dark housetops and silent streets. Lamp-posts pointed grotesque fingers at the sky. Davis looked at the sky. A huge yellow moon swam majestically through white clouds. Hundreds, millions, of clean white stars peered untwinkling out of an eternity of space. And behind the clouds, moon and stars was everlasting vastness.

A deluge of memories swept along the channels of his brain, and as if a dozen dams, overstrained by pressure, had broken, the channels overflowed, joined forces ever increasingly and flooded his mind.

Suddenly he remembered those great white moments of his life which he knew were his best ones: the day he stood among the chauffeurs and saw Tom carried about the field in triumph; the night he had kissed Margie's hand and called her sweetheart; that afternoon of impelling sensations and thrills when Johnnie Walker was coming to the front; that instant of catching Margie's eye as Alvin led the winner through the cheering crowd to the paddock; and now this magnificent moment when he looked out over the housetops and streets.

With a feeling that might have been Samson's as he reached for the pillars of the Philistine temple, Davis Pettigrier turned from the window, strode to the door, down the steps, and out into the night. He went back to Varsity Avenue, past the Owl Club, past the Baptist church to his own room. And that night he slept a dreamless, healing sleep which had not been his for many months.

XX

People would tell you that Jackson Pettigrier was a fortunate man. He had come to Cranston twenty-five years ago almost a pauper. He had stepped into a good position at the bank, risen rapidly, won a much-courted bride, and gone on steadily to prosperity and success. Now he was president of a big company, lived in a country house with his still beautiful wife, was blessed with a dutiful son, and regarded and respected as a useful citizen. He was a good man and, by all the laws of logic and justice, should have been a happy one, people would say.

Yet he was not happy and the sight of John Lucas' check for ten thousand dollars did not tend to make him so. He was sorry that Lucas was able to repay him on the first day of June according to their bond. Last month a western millionaire had driven away with Lucas' daughter. Three weeks later Lucas paid the debt. Four weeks later he was indicted for fraud against the government.

Mr. Pettigrier was not given to jumping at unpleasant conclusions. Still, when one had only to read the stock quotations to see Grafton Chemicals falling away to worthlessness; when everyone in Cranston knew that the day after Mr. and Mrs. Schnell left on their honeymoon John Lucas had advertised his house for sale, when the papers were full of the case of the United States against John Lucas, what was a man to believe?

Mr. Pettigrier laughed bitterly at his own delicacy. He had winced at the fear that Lucas might think he had ulterior motives for making the loan. He had

143

thought Lucas too high a type to consider money and his own flesh and blood in the same moment of thought.   Now he realized that for that very consideration Lucas had approached him, had used his daughter to catch the loan, and, finding the bait would do for bigger game, had used it again. He had sold a valuable possession to the highest bidder. Mr. Pettigrier thought him a blackguard, but with the inconsistency of outraged decency fervently wished that he had been that bidder.

There was some ironic compensation in the fact that the debt being paid, he could take Davis and Molly to Europe this summer.   Heaven knows, they both needed it, he thought. He wondered how the boy had stood the double shock of Margie's marriage and the club disappointment. He gauged his son's feelings by his own. Mr. Pettigrier's pride and paternal affection had suffered grievously under both blows. He hoped Davis would be courageous enough to rally and go on to success and happiness, but he was not at all sure. Early defeat leaves great gaps in a man's self-confidence. Yes, it was fortunate that the trip was possible.   Perhaps change of environment would give the boy fresh strength.

And Molly, too, needed a change. She had fallen into a strange nervous disorder lately, a kind of morbid melancholia. She was not at all herself. Only last Sunday when Alvin was there she had made a scene by suddenly leaving the table in a burst of tears. Alvin, of course, was an old friend, but still one does not like that sort of thing before outsiders—not to mention the servants. Yes, he thought, the trip would do Molly good, too.

Aboard the steamship *Urania* bound for Naples, Davis sat bundled and propped up in a deck chair reading *Tess of the D'Urbervilles*. It was deliciously peaceful on shipboard. Those two years at college had taxed his vitality. It seemed to him he was always tired, always anxious for a chance to forget to think. His college career seemed now like one long day. He hardly knew what events belonged to each year. Had Margie married before or after the Damp episode? Had Tom left him this year or last? He did not want to know. All that mattered was that these things had happened and would never happen in the same way again. Every twist of the big propeller was driving him farther away. Every bit of foam that dropped astern was that much more between him and the past. He was glad of it.

He sat at table with his parents and sometimes he walked about the deck with one or both of them, but most of the time he was alone. Long ago he had acquired the habit of reading oblivious to environment. People who strolled past his chair chatting and laughing he scarcely noticed.

On the third night out, there was dancing as usual in the saloon. Davis paused at the doorway, book in hand, as a familiar tune caught his attention:

"Oh Mr. Shean, Mr. Shean,
    Exercising in the bathroom's quite a scheme,
    But be sure and have a care, if there's a radiator
        there.
    Suppose there is one, Mr. Gallagher!
    Be sure and face it, Mr. Shean."

It was that catchy ragtime that you heard everywhere in 1923. The last time Davis remembered having heard it was that Monday in March when the postman whistled it outside his door. He smiled ruefully.

Someone jostled him from behind and he realized he was blocking the entrance. He moved aside with an apology, making room for the pair of dancers.

The girl was pretty, he noticed indifferently, rather the type Phil would have called "tangible." Dark, with her hair parted and slicked back; slim, with a green satin evening dress clinging voluptuously to her frame; smiling, with her eyes half-closed and her lips barely touching. It was only a cursory glance he allowed her as he flattened out against the wall to let them pass. It is possible he would never have thought of her again had she not, brushing by with a scented rustling, said,

"Thank you, Davis Pettigrier."

He followed her with his eyes. He saw her dancing close to her partner's shoulder. Not the slightest glimmer of recognition did she recall. He changed his mind about reading in the library and instead took a chair against the saloon wall, where he examined the dark dancer from all angles. His interest increased with his curiosity. Finally, late in the evening he approached a man who had just finished a dance with her.

"I've met her, but I can't remember the name," Davis said carelessly.

The man's reply was of little importance as the name was no more familiar than her face. "Alice Dupres of New York."

The next morning when Davis sought his deck chair it was not for literary reasons. He was lying in ambush, with what purpose he hardly knew. He did know that if he had sat there long enough he would be almost certain to have another sight of Alice Dupres, but what to do with the opportunity when he got it he could not say.

Surely enough, about eleven o'clock she came in sight at the far end of the deck, bearing down swiftly on him. Pretending to read till she had passed, he looked up. Davis misjudged the distance, however, perhaps because Miss Dupres slowed down consider-

ably as she came abreast his chair. He misjudged the
distance and as he raised his eyes they looked straight
into hers.

She nodded, said "Good-morning" and, suddenly
resuming her former speed, sailed smartly out of
sight around the corner.

Davis squirmed uncomfortably and closed his book.
At the rate she was going it would not be long before
she circled the deck and passed again. Mechanically
he straightened his cravat and smoothed down his
hair. He wouldn't go one step out of his way either
to meet or to avoid her. If she kept following him
around, it certainly was not his fault.

Here she came again, her skirts blown taut against
her, her chin tilted to the breeze. She minced along
like an exuberant two-year-old feeling its strength
for the first time. Again their lines of sight crossed.

They both smiled and instantly, veering in her
course, she came straight toward him. Flinging off
the blanket and dropping the book, he stood up.

"You don't remember me," she said.

"Oh, yes, I do. You're Alice Dupres from New
York. I met you at the Kingston prom."

"Noble effort," she laughed, "but you're wrong;
that is, all but the name and address. I've never been
to Kingston, but last April I did go to the races at
Madingly. I saw you win and congratulated you
afterwards, only you don't remember."

"Yes, now I do—won't you sit down?"

"Thanks," she said, and took Mrs. Pettigrier's chair,
which was next to his.

Davis danced with Alice that evening. She wore
pink this time and it showed the same clinging tendency
that green had the evening before. Mr. and Mrs.
Pettigrier came into the saloon for coffee. His mother
beckoned Davis as he left his partner.

"Davis, who is that girl you just danced with?

Someone ought to tell her to wear more clothes. Why don't you meet some nice girls?"

"She is a nice girl, mother. Alice Dupres of New York."

Mrs. Pettigrier looked nervous and drawn. Her color was bad and there was a whine of petulance in her voice. She was losing her beauty.

"No nice girl dresses like that, Davis. Just look at her legs. It's positively vulgar."

Davis had been looking before she mentioned legs, but now he looked away. He did not dance with Alice again till his parents had retired. Alice insisted that he tell her all about the race and they made an engagement for the next day. He saw her to the door of her cabin that night.

The next morning he told her all about the race. That afternoon they played shuffle-board and had tea together. That evening they met again on the dance floor. She had reverted to green, and it became her better for the repetition. Davis regretted his own procrastination in meeting her. He had wasted three whole days and there were only eight more. She was charming to look on and apt in conversation. Once he caught himself applying the adjective he had so often used for Margie—wonderful.

Early in the evening he danced with her.

"Well, young man, aren't you ever going to ask me to sit out, or must I ask you?"

"Oh, let's do. I was just going to ask you."

"I'll run down and get my shawl so we can go outside."

She returned with her shoulders draped and her vivacious little head looking all the more vivacious for seeming to stick out of a bag. They walked the deck for a while. The wind seemed to blow her against him whether she walked on the inside or out.

The mere walking of the main deck soon became

tiresome. There was a staircase leading down to B deck. They went down.

"Let's sit on the steps a while," Alice suggested.

They sat and talked. Davis told her several hunting anecdotes. In the middle of one she said:

"It's cold."

"Do you want to go in?" he said politely, but she wrapped the shawl closer and did not answer. In spite of her care the wrap would not keep its place properly. Davis chivalrously lent a hand, and in doing so he suddenly found his voice becoming hushed and husky.

"Oh, now," she exclaimed, as he withdrew the helping hand, "I've something in my eye."

Once again he was pressed into service and with the corner of his handkerchief searched for the offending particle. This required close scrutiny and their heads at one moment were almost tangent. At this moment the shawl required attention.

Davis for the first time in his life held a girl in his arms. He felt reckless, timorous, ashamed, all at once. He let his right arm remain over her shoulder and looked into her eyes expecting to find there a reprimand. The reprimand had been there all evening, but it was gone now.

Her head dropped on to his shoulder, her weight rested against his right arm. He felt weak, dizzy, foolish, helpless. It was not a totally unfamiliar feeling, except for its intensity. His other arm he slipped under her waist and, crushing her to him, he kissed her.

In spite of his mother's disapproval, Davis spent practically all his waking hours of the next few days with Alice. He found her the most delightful of companions. One starry evening they sat on the boat deck propped up against the railing.

"Alice, have you ever been in love before?"

She wrinkled her pert little nose.

"Have you?" she asked cautiously.

"No," said Davis, "only once I almost thought I was."

"I've thought so myself once or twice," she answered.

Davis looked sideways at her. He wished the captain would drop anchor here somewhere off Gibraltar and never weigh. This week was going as the old school holidays used to go. Three more days and they would land at Naples. She would go one way and he another. Davis sighed.

"I believe people only love once in a lifetime. There's one girl for every man in the world. Plato said so two thousand years ago. Did you ever read Plato?"

She never had, and neither had Davis, although he had read about him.

Alice still maintained her pensive attitude and, when he turned towards her, Davis saw only her profile artfully silhouetted against the darkness.

"I knew the first time I saw you that you were the only girl for me. I've seen lots of girls, but I knew right away you were different."

She faced him, all softness and witchery.

"How do you mean 'different'?" she asked deftly, like an angler flicking his fly across the water.

"I knew you were the only girl in the world I could ever love."

"I'll bet," she said archly, "when we land I'll never see you again."

"Didn't you promise to come to the prom next winter? Have you forgotten already?"

"No, but you will before the time comes. I always wanted to go to a Kingston prom. I know lots of men there. Do you know one named Johnson—Bob Johnson—in the Owl Club?"

Davis winced.

"Slightly. Is he a friend of yours?"

"Oh, a great friend. You ought to know him better. He's a great fellow."

Davis seemed to lose interest in the conversation. He got up and leaned over the rail, listening to the splashing of the waves against the ship. Soon they went below and parted.

Alone in his cabin, Davis sat disconsolately on the edge of his bed and thought of the vanity of human wishes. For four golden days he had known happiness, the careless, thoughtless happiness that should belong to youth. Now he saw he must lose it again and forever. The mention of Johnson brought back all his sense of loneliness. How could he ever hope to do and enjoy things that his contemporaries did, he who was an outcast among them? How, for instance, could he think of having Alice to a prom when he had hardly a friend at college?

He pulled off a shoe and let it drop. He should have known better than to try to be happy. What would Alice think of him when Johnson told her all?

The next morning the *Urania* slipped indolently into the Mediterranean. Davis had looked forward to this event. He had thought to find pleasure in soliloquizing about this sea of lovers. He had meant to stand on the boat deck with Alice and think that perhaps he was looking over the same waves that Anthony had with Cleopatra beside him. When the occasion for these soliloquies came the mood had passed and Davis had returned to the deck chair and book.

The three remaining days on board were as uneventful as the first three had been. Davis met Alice's advances with coolness and returned them with indifference. Hour after hour he would sit hunched up in his deck chair doggedly reading. He took satisfaction in Alice's meek but evident distress, imagining himself the avenger of his sex which had suffered so much from hers. If he were tempted to put aside his sulkiness and enjoy the romance while it lasted, he would remind himself that as soon as Alice learned of him from Johnson she would despise him and sever their relations immediately. He preferred to do the severing himself while it was in his power to do so.

The intensity of her son's interest and its sudden dissipation was not lost on Mrs. Pettigrier. It irritated her that Davis had ignored her wishes in the first instance. She told her husband that Davis would surely turn out a prodigal. She pointed out an undeniable Pettigrier weakness for sins of the flesh and called up as evidence the shades of several profligate Pettigriers.

Jackson Pettigrier, husband and father, was nettled. He could not deny that some of his more distant ancestors had led free lives, but that Molly should insist on unpleasant subjects was annoying. She had not been herself for several months now. One had to be patient with her. The sea voyage had not had the soothing effect he had hoped for, but traveling on the continent must certainly inspire her interest and dispel her melancholy he thought.

When Davis first showed signs of being sensible to the charms of Alice, his father had been pleased. He considered it unnatural for a boy of twenty to be alone as much as Davis preferred to be. Jackson Pettigrier remembered his own youth as a time of hot-blooded friendships and loves. He would never have been content to read books while there was beauty, music and romance all in the narrow confines of a ship at sea. He was glad when Davis laid by his book and disappeared to dark decks with Alice Dupres.

Meanwhile the captain of the *Urania,* insensible to the emotions of his passengers, steered straight for

Naples, and docked his ship. Davis Pettigrier stepped onto a foreign soil, possessed of the same puzzled soul with which he had stepped off his native one. Happiness had been his only a few days and that had been in no country, but on the ownerless sea.

XXI

The Pettigriers saw Italy from over the shoulder and under the elbows of those children of curiosity, the tourists. Naples, Venice, Florence, Rome, pictures, buildings, catacombs, ruins. Hot trains, cold meals, aching legs, weary eyes. Mr. Pettigrier with provincial simplicity praised everything indiscriminately, but personally he would rather have been sitting over a mint julep on his own veranda, or talking to Alvin at the club. This wasn't his trip, he told himself, it was for Molly and Davis. If they enjoyed themselves he would be satisfied.

Davis found enthusiasm for many things. Especially for Rome. Rome, the Eternal City, the prize for which Marius and Sulla and Cæsar and Pompey had each other's throats. The very dust that made him cough had choked the citizens who came out to cheer an emperor's triumph. Within walls that still stood Roman mothers had quieted their children with "Hannibal ad portas."

And the people themselves: that olive-throated fruit-vendor, for instance. Who can say that his ancestors had not fallen at Pharsalia or the siege of Capua? Perhaps that glowering policeman dressed like a soldier was only the living descendant of the admiral who threw his portentous chickens overboard because they would not grant him an omen of victory.

For three weeks they stayed in Italy, then they went to Paris. By this time the novelty of travel had worn off. Davis tried to arouse himself over Paris as he had over Rome. These were the streets whose paving stones had been ramparts in the revolution. Over this ground had strode Henri of Navarre, he of the white plume. Napoleon had been cheered within these same shadows. But Davis was unmoved. Heroes and courtiers may have lived there, but it was no city of heroes and courtiers today. It was one of shrieking taxicabs and rubbernecked tourists. Except for a day at the battlefields he was bored. He begged to be excused from visiting the Louvre and the Luxemburg. For the first few days they made him accompany them to places on the guide book list, but soon despairing, they left him to amuse himself, which he did with a book in his room.

One sultry afternoon having read himself drowsy, he decided to take a walk. He stepped into the elevator at the fourth floor. At the third a slim lady, dressed in her Parisian best stepped in. Davis gasped.

"Good Lord, Margie, how are you?"

Instead of going for a walk he had tea with Margie. Roswell was downtown on business she explained. They had only arrived this morning from a trip that was the last leg of their honeymoon. They were sailing home tomorrow.

Davis had not seen her since that night in February when he had fought with Tom. She looked remarkably unchanged. There was nothing matronly about her serge suit and jaunty felt hat.

"Well, Margie, how do you like being married? We miss you terribly at home."

"Oh, Dave, you don't know how anxious I am to see my new home in Cincinnati. It wasn't finished when I saw it last April. My, but I'll miss Cranston! Didn't we used to have some times? Remember Sunday nights at our house when father used to chase everyone out at ten-thirty?"

"Do I? Remember when I was suspended from school and we used to go to the movies every afternoon, Margie—or must I call you Mrs. Schnell?"

They both laughed. Margie looked up and said, "Here comes Roswell."

Davis stood up and shook hands with her husband. "Hello there, Pettigrier. Long way from home, I'll say."

Roswell Schnell evidently had flourished on foreign cooking. His jowls were baggy with fat and two buttons on his waistcoat were under considerable strain. When he sat down at the little round table opposite his wife, he did it by abandoning his body to the laws of gravitation and landing on the chair to all appearances merely by chance. Davis noticed that his nails and hands were none too clean. There was, too, thought the younger man, an unmistakable odor of perspiration and damp linen.

"Well, Marge, did a nice piece of business this after. Got a contract that ought to run into big figures. Nothing like combining business with pleasure, Pettigrier. Get out and hustle all the time. That's why I never went to college. Waste of time, I say. Time is money. You wouldn't waste money, would you? Then why waste time?"

"That's right," Davis admitted.

Margie was serenely pouring tea. She passed Schnell a cup, which he motioned aside with an imperial gesture.

"Tea! Take it away. Hot water was made to shave with. Let's have something fit to drink. I drink all I can while I can get good stuff. It's dirt cheap over here, too. What'll it be, Pettigrier? I'll have a *side-car*. Waiter, two *side-cars*. Tell him in French, Marge, and have one yourself. Make it three."

Margie and Davis declared they preferred tea at the moment.

"Keep it, waiter, keep the change," boomed the plutocratic bridegroom, dropping a ten franc note on the tray as he lifted off the cocktail. "It's only fifty cents in real money."

The Schnells insisted that Davis dine with them and go to a theatre that night.

"These night clubs are the real thing, Pettigrier. We've been to all the big ones, Zelli's, Florence's, the Casino—but I like the Red Cow best of all. At least, that's what it means, only the French have some other name for it. We'll take in the Red Cow tonight."

Davis dressed slowly that evening, putting in his shirt studs with cold, nervous fingers. He had never dreamed of seeing Margie in Paris. He had thought, perhaps, never to see her again, at least not for years. Yet here she was. The same irresponsible lovely Margie with brown wispy hair and divinely pug nose. Dreamily he fumbled with his black bow-tie. Margie, whom he had loved in Cranston, he had met in Paris. In Paris, on her honeymoon with Schnell. Savagely he tugged, squaring the corners of his tie. He had cut his chin with the razor. He borrowed some face powder from his mother and dabbed the tiny scar.

La Vache Rouge was just gathering momentum when they arrived about half-past twelve. Roswell Schnell had reserved a table. As they sat down the lights were lowered and a purple spotlight escorted to the center of the floor a young lady whose costume suggested nakedness rather than a covering. She sang a French ditty and tripped a whirling, kicking measure to appreciative applause. The lights went on, the orchestra crashed into an American fox trot. Davis asked Margie to dance.

"It's been a long time since we danced, Margie. At least, lots of things have happened since then."

"I'm furious you didn't come down to the wedding. Everyone was there."

The floor was very crowded and Margie hugged his shoulder to keep from being jostled. He could see the downy fuzz on her cheek like the fuzz on a ripe peach.

"Look, Margie, look over there!"

Margie looked.   A jet black negro was dancing gawkily about with a French "hostess."

"Oh," laughed Margie.   "You'll have to get used to that over here."

"I never will.   He ought to be thrown out, the big black chauffeur!"

He noticed the dancers about him.   There were painted, hollow-eyed women with young college men; pretty girls pretending to be merry with corpulent men of forty.   At least seventy-five per cent of the male guests were American.   Davis was surprised, although he hardly knew what he had expected.

Margie was saying she would be glad to get home, that he must visit them in Cincinnati.

"Tell me about Cranston," she said.   "How did you leave them all, Tom and Phil, and Tillie and Lou?"

Davis complied, wondering that she never asked about her own father and mother.   He wondered if she knew of the pending trial.   She must.

The music stopped and returning to the table they found that Roswell had ordered champagne.   Roswell had indulged copiously at dinner and during the *entre acts* at the theatre.   He was sleepy and yawned.

"When I get back to Cincinnati," he murmured, "I'll get twelve hours every night.   Enough of this kind of life is enough.   No place like home."

Conversation with Margie was not easy in her husband's presence; and as that fortunate man did not care to dance, Davis took the opportunities himself. He had never drunk any quantity of champagne before and the stuff had a quickening effect.   No longer did he mind the jostling crowd.   His feet were lightened, his tongue was loosened.   He was enjoying himself.

"Well," said Roswell, scrutinizing his watch from

under heavy eyelids, "its two-thirty, and I'm going to bed. If you kids want to stay, all right. Marge," handing her his wallet, "you settle the bill and come home when you get ready."

He was gone. Davis filled his own glass and Margie's. She put her elbows on the table and smiled. They drank their champagne and danced again. Davis thought of the many times he had put his arm around her waist, and never once without a conscious thrill. Weaving in and out among the other couples, he exulted in this bit of luck. Who could have told him that he would ever live to enjoy such happiness again?

By their appearance they were the youngest persons there. Freshness and loveliness of youth seemed personified in their dancing. It was

> "like young delight
> Gone courting April maidenhood,
> That has the primrose in her blood."

Hard-mouthed French "hostesses" trying to entertain their besotted customers looked at the pair wistfully.

Margie was gay, gayer, thought Davis, than he had ever seen her. She was almost coquettish. She drank sparingly and smoked a great deal.

"Remember, Margie, the first time you told me you smoked?"

"Remember, Dave, when we used to skate at night-time?"

"And dancing class?"

"And Johnnie Walker, Dave! My, I was excited! You were a hero. Weren't they the days?"

"Only a year ago, too, Margie. Seems longer."

"Much longer, Dave. Promise me you will come to Cincinnati and see me."

They danced. It was half-past three, half-past four. Davis' wildness of joy had softened into a mellowness. They sat and talked.

"I'll never get married, Margie."

"Why not, Dave?"

"Oh, I don't know."

Five o'clock.

"We ought to go," she said.

She had said so before, but this time they did.   In the taxi she put her arm through his.   The fur on the collar of her opera cloak touched his cheek.

It was grey between the buildings and down the side streets.

"Reminds me of cub-hunting, being up this early," he said.   "You know, Margie, I've still got that snapshot you gave me to carry in the race.   I suppose now you're Mrs. Schnell I ought to give it back."

He looked at her.   There was enough light to see her face plainly.   She was weeping gently.

XXII

Alvin Martin was a jealous man. He envied other
men to whom fate had given great moments. He
envied John Paul Jones the opportunity of standing
on the bridge of the *Bonhomme Richard* and shouting,
"We haven't begun to fight yet." He envied Farragut,
the chance of saying "Damn the torpedoes," and Lord
Nelson for being given the combination of a blind eye
and a signal to retreat. He was even jealous of the
poor Christian gladiators who used to walk up to the
emperor's box and say with a grand flourish, *"Mori-
tari salutamus!"*

He had always been on the lookout for such chances.
In France during the War he was forever planning
gestures, but nothing ever came of it. Small room
was there for heroics standing knee-deep in mud
or creeping on one's belly through strands of barbed
wire. He had thought of joining the cavalry, but all
the cavalry seemed to do was to act as traffic police.
He wished he had lived in the middle ages when men
knew how to fight a war.

As a boy he had dreamed of being a statesman and
of routing his opposition with invincible rhetoric.
One day his father took him to Washington and to
Congress. Instead of breath-taking flights of oratory
and thunderstorms of applause, there was only a big
room half full of seedy-looking men, some reading
newspapers, some chatting, some drowsing, while one
law maker was doggedly reciting a speech of which no
syllable reached young Alvin's ears although they were
hanging well out over the balcony railing. That experience had stifled all his political ambitions.

By the time he had finished college Alvin had come

to the opinion that life was more like a railroad wait-
ing-room than anything else.   Men sat there waiting
for their train.   They all had a long wait and less bored
the man who found something to amuse himself.   If
Alvin ever prayed it was for some kind of excitement
to dispel the boredom of his waiting.   He fox-hunted
and steeple-chased.   That is exciting on occasions, but
mildly so.   He tried the Great War and found it on the
whole less thrilling than racing.   It was too depressing,
never letting one forget that he was in the waiting
room with everybody else's train coming but one's
own.

Alvin had become a lawyer in self-defense.   The
profession gave him a certain amount of competitive
thinking, which he enjoyed immensely.   He reveled in
a match of wits.   He was never so pleased as when he
could entice some of the men at the club into an argument.   He loved to snort at their banal statements, to
scandalize them with his unconventional theories and
contemptuous epigrams.   Above all he loved his own
epigrams.

Seldom and sweet were the chances of indulging
these fancies of his in a professional way.   A few
years ago there had been a case tried at Cranston in
which some mountaineers from an outlying district
were accused of treason for resisting the enforcement
of a constitutional amendment.   Alvin was counsel for
the defense.   He had made a public laughing stock and
a life-long enemy of the prosecuting attorney.   The
prisoners were dismissed for lack of evidence.

Alvin despaired of ever getting a case like that again.
He tried to reconcile himself to another long wait.   His
one hope had been that the district attorney would
challenge him to a fight or at least sue him for libel.
But that hope soon vanished.   It seemed there was
only an infinity of undiluted boredom ahead, bore-

dom he could only endure with the help of his horses, his books and a few unwary dupes at the club.

Then down from the north came John Lucas and Alvin became attorney for Grafton Chemicals. There were a few civil cases, typically boring. One day Lucas came to him personally for legal advice. In the course of a year he came back for more than advice for he had been indicted on the charge of defrauding the federal government. It had to do with the war-time contract by which Lucas had made his fortune. The trial was set for September of 1923.

It would be nothing but unnecessary and uninteresting repetition to go into the case of the *United States against John Lucas,* even if that were possible. It is enough to say here that Alvin considered it one of the greatest events in his life. Never before had he found his brain more active, his wits sharper. He pounced upon quibbles and turned them into defensive bulwarks. He got a lever into every legal crevice in the statute books and widened it into a loophole. He came out from behind his walls to make spirited sallies at the besiegers. He threw off epigrams worthy of Pope, eloquence worthy of Mark Anthony. He chaffed the opposition, scoffed at their evidence, snorted at their accusations. He mimicked the state's attorney and was fined for contempt of court.

Bowing with the elegance of a cavalier he apologized, hoped the court would forgive his enthusiasm, hoped the prosecution would not misinterpret his motives. He was only pleading for justice, that is, legal justice, gentlemen of the jury. He was sure they were all one on that point. He quibbled, he canted, he juggled phrases of the contract.

In the end, John Lucas was acquitted of the charge. Everybody in the courtroom knew he was morally guilty—Alvin had never denied that—but legally he was an honest man. The next day he declared himself bankrupt, and continued to live, as he had for several months, in a small apartment on his wife's money. He had sold his house, his cars, and a great deal of furniture. What money and property he had left after the failure of Grafton Chemicals, he had deeded over to his wife before the trial. When Alvin received a cheque covering his fee, it was signed "Martha Lucas."

People in Cranston were kind to Mrs. Lucas. "After all," said the ladies who called on her and invited her out, "after all, any of us might just as well have married a crook. You can't hold a woman responsible for her husband the way you can a man for his wife. It's a different matter."

Cranston, in fact, was quite puffed up about the whole affair. Here two of her citizens had become national figures over night. The Cranston *Exponent* printed several editorials by way of a panegyric on Alvin. They ran a picture of him on Johnnie Walker in the Sunday paper. One day a committee called at Alvin's office. They wanted to know if he would care to go to Congress.

"No, thanks," said Alvin. "I've been."

XXIII

The day before Davis left Cranston for Kingston that autumn, Tom Stevension called him on the telephone. Tom wanted to know what train Davis was taking. He suggested that they return together. It was quite plainly an attempt at reconciliation. Davis at first was inclined to reject it in pride, but a fast-following after-thought, carrying with it images of a lonely window seat, made him humble.

"I'll meet you on the five-ten, Tom. Phil and Joe have gone, haven't they?"

It was a five-hour ride to Kingston. When they first opened conversation there were several times when both were thinking of one thing and talking of another. They avoided unpleasant subjects with awkward circumlocutions, but by the time they had changed trains at Washington and were comfortably fed, the strain had lessened.

"Saw Margie in Paris. She and Schnell stayed at the same hotel."

"Well, I should think they would now they're married."

"I mean they stayed at the same hotel that we did. Schnell's a funny one, isn't he?"

"You never did think much of him, did you, Dave?"

"Oh, I don't know. Must be a pretty good fellow, or Margie wouldn't have taken him."

"Phil says the reason she did was—," Tom checked himself, but it was too late.

"Phil talks too much, I think."

"Same here," said Tom quickly.

Davis found that the renewal of relations with Tom made a great difference in his life at college. During

165

that autumn they came to wander in and out of each other's rooms with all the freedom of friendship. Davis even came to see redeeming qualities in Johnson. Tom, Phil and Joe asked him to the Owl Club for dinner several times, but these were not the occasions that Davis particularly enjoyed. He always felt as if the other members were discussing him.

He came to spend more and more time with Dr. Down. The old man with his deep feeling for English poetry grew on Davis. They spent many an evening together, reading aloud in turn. From his other friends in the faculty Davis began to fall away. He found that after their first revolutionary harangues Professors Harvey and Redmond had little to give him except repetition and illustrations of their theories. Davis was sick of theories and abstractions, tired of thinking, arguing, and quibbling. He did not know exactly what it was he craved, but he felt increasingly confident that Dr. Down was giving it to him.

He often wondered what he would do about his promise to Alice concerning the prom. They still corresponded in a desultory way and it was plain from her letters that she considered the invitation open. If Johnson had told her disagreeable things about him she did not seem affected by them. Davis had made up his mind that he would not go through the ordeal of having her down. That was settled; but how and by what methods he was going to rid himself of her was still an open question. Phil advised that he simply stop writing to her. That would sever relations effectively enough, but Davis would not be rude. His southern blood revolted at the thought of hurting a lady's feelings. There must be some other way. He decided to wait and see whether circumstance would not settle the matter for him. The prom was over three months off. Anything might happen in that time.

Davis persuaded himself that since he had seen

Margie he had lost all interest in Alice. He berated himself for even thinking that he could love anyone but Margie. How he ever could have allowed himself to lavish upon Alice the self-same terms of endearment that had belonged to his first love was beyond his conception. These sacred syllables were now stored up for sentimental gloatings, never again to be profaned by use. Margie was lost so far as any hope of possession was concerned, but he would love her and only her to the end of his days.

As the term advanced, Davis' work continued to be highly satisfactory. He became the pride of the English department when one of his essays received first prize in an open competition. Dr. Down was elated. He told Davis that he should consider teaching as a profession. There was a scholarship open at the graduate school, he hinted.

Mr. Pettigrier was very proud of the essay. When Davis came home for Christmas his father listened earnestly to what the young man had to say.

"Dr. Down is on the committee. He says I'm almost sure to get the scholarship if I apply; and if I do well with it I can get a job teaching at Kingston."

"Well, son, I always had it in my mind that you would be a physician. It's nothing but a whim of mine, though, and we have almost two years to think it over. You can be certain I won't interfere with any of your ambitions."

"What do you want him to be a doctor for, Jackson?" Alvin put in. "You think they save people's lives, but they don't. They only postpone death a little while.

'A day less or more at sea or shore
We die—does it matter when?'

Who wrote that, professor?"
Davis did not know.

"Hardly a fair question, I reckon," Alvin continued. "A very obscure writer named Tennyson—used to be poet laureate of England."

"One reason against his teaching is that it would take him away from home. If he decided to become a doctor he could take his degree at the State University and then practice in Cranston. I built this house and I like to think that after I'm gone a Pettigrier will live here."

Mrs. Pettigrier was arranging flowers in a vase by the window. Without turning her head she answered her husband:

"Oh, Jackson, I never heard such sentimental nonsense. Who cares what happens to this old house? And as for wanting to keep the boy at home, that's worse. Why didn't you stay home? Because you wanted to succeed—which you wouldn't have done if you had sat around your father's house?"

"I know, Molly, but this case is different. It was necessary for me to get out and feed myself. I've made it possible for Davis to have more advantages than I had. I'd like the name of Pettigrier to mean something in a community and it won't if Davis is a professor, no matter how clever he is. Besides I hate to see good southern stock taking root up there in Yankee land. And again, I want him to live with us always."

"There isn't much chance of that, Jackson. He'll be married soon and have his own home."

"If Davis is half the man I think he is," interposed Alvin, "he'll know better than to get married.

'While horses are horses to train and to race
The women and wine take second place.'

Here's another chance for you, professor. I'll bet

you on a race for Johnnie Walker, you don't even know who wrote that."

"Saddle up your race horse, Alvin.   That was written by an obscure young fellow named Kipling."

XXIV

It was late in January. Davis sprawled on his window seat. It was dark outside. Nine o'clock just struck in the frosty tower of Putnam Hall. Davis felt the wind slipping through the crevices of the window casement. He drew the curtain, moved to the armchair before the fire and put on some more wood.

For the first time in his life Davis felt that he knew something about the way of the world; felt that experience had untaught him most of the abstract fallacies he had learned in boyhood.

For instance, his old code had said that it was impossible for him to live without Margie. Yet he seemed to be getting on well enough. In fact, Davis thought, most of his success had come after he had lost Margie —certainly most of his wisdom had. In his first two years at Kingston he had lost what friends he had come up with and had failed to make any new ones. His associates had been poor Richard Damp and the Lincoln Society members. This year he had recovered his old friends and made several new ones. If Margie had married in freshman year, he thought, probably he would have been elected to the Owl Club.

Besides the raising of his social status, he had achieved a small literary success. The prize essay was no mean accomplishment for his first attempt. Since then he had had accepted by the *Campus* two book reviews. He was no longer the laughing-stock of the college, but a respected citizen.

Davis thrust his toes toward the blaze. He was pleased with life this evening. Things had gone well all year. He liked his work and excelled in it. Practically nothing had happened or threatened to interrupt the smoothness of existence. He would make more friends and write more reviews this winter. When spring came he would ride Johnnie Walker.

Only one matter tended to disquiet him. That was the matter of Alice and the prom. It was only a month off and she still expected to come. Nothing had happened to get him out of this predicament. He had counted on circumstance offering him an escape. So far it had not. He wondered, sliding deeper into his chair and balancing one heel on the andiron, he wondered lethargically whether it would. He was no longer much concerned. It was, he thought, too small a thing to challenge his happiness.

Alvin had said the only happy man was a drunken one. Davis felt that he was doing fairly well for a sober man. This was what Dr. Peckam was always talking about—"the peace that passeth understanding." He smiled into the fireplace.

There was a knocking at the door. One of his new friends, thought Davis, his old ones never knocked.

"Telegram, sir."

Davis tipped the messenger and tore open the yellow envelope.

> "Your mother is seriously ill with pneumonia. Come down at once.
>
> Father"

He read it twice over. His mother with pneumonia! He had known that she was in bed with a cold—but pneumonia!

He stood leaning on the table with his fists. There were no trains going south from Kingston at this time of night. He went across the hall. Nobody there. He put on his overcoat and ran over the campus to Phil's room. Phil would know what to do. There was a sharp wind blowing. It made his eyes water.

Phil was in. He was working at his desk with a green eyeshade on his forehead. He scowled as Davis bolted in. Phil hated being disturbed at his work and showed it plainly, but he swore sympathetically when Davis explained.

"What you got to do, Dave, is to go to New York and then take the midnight for Washington. That'll get you there about six in the morning. You can catch an early train for Cranston. Got any money?"

"Not much," said Davis helplessly.

Phil emptied his wallet.

"Five dollars. That won't do. Wait here."

He hurried out of the room, and Davis left alone lit one of Phil's cigarettes. He walked about the room not caring to sit down. His head was full of spinning, whirling thoughts. He felt only a semi-consciousness.

Phil reappeared in ten minutes and put a handful of banknotes on the table.

"Twenty-five dollars. That'll see you through. Take it and take this, too." He took two unopened packages of cigarettes from a drawer. "You'll need them. It's a long ride."

Davis pocketed everything without a syllable.

Phil was getting into his overcoat and gloves.

"I'm going with you to New York and put you on the sleeper. Don't argue. Come on. We can just make the nine-forty."

Phil did not press conversation during the ninety minutes ride to New York. He asked only practical questions. What time had the telegram come? Had Davis wired an answer? They went to the information booth in the Pennsylvania Station to find out about trains from Washington to Cranston. After a great deal of swearing Phil found there was one at six-thirty-two.

"You'll be home for breakfast, Dave, and probably you'll find things not as bad as you think."

"Why don't I telephone from here?" Davis suggested.

Phil was against this.

"You'll only disturb the house," he said.

They sent a telegram stating the time of arrival. Phil saw Davis to his berth.

"Now try and get some sleep. If you can't, go in the smoking room and smoke yourself dizzy. Don't lie here and think, whatever you do. So long, Dave, and let's hope it won't be so bad after all."

Davis thanked him duly for all he had done. Phil ignored the thanks, shook hands and ran to catch his own train back to Kingston.

Davis took off his coat, waistcoat and shoes and lay down in his berth. He was still conscious of a total lack of emotion. Everything in him seemed impotent. He could think now, but he could not feel.

He knew that Mrs. Pettigrier must be desperately ill, else his father would never have sent such a message. He found himself assuming that she would die, assuming it grimly and without grief. He tried to imagine the changes her death would cause at home. He thought first of his father. There was bitterness in the thought. His father would suffer most. This thing would change him greatly. It was the noblest who suffered most in this world, just as Alvin always said.

Still assuming a fatal conclusion Davis wondered what difference it would make in his own life. He was not attached to his mother as he was to his father. He loved her, of course, and when she was gone he would miss her just as he had missed Margie—only much more.

The thought of Margie seemed incongruous at such a time. Like a great wave breaking up a tired swimmer, came the realization that this was death he was thinking of. Death was not like anything else in the world. It was more than a parting, more than a missing of people. Death was the falling into the bottomless pit. It was the listening to a clapperless bell. It was terrible, mysterious and cruel. And his mother was dying. Not going away, not going to sleep or to heaven, but she was dying. He realized at that moment the insipidity, the futility of all synonyms for death. Death, the word, meant one thing so completely. And death was coming to his mother. Another incongruous thought spun in: Now he would not have to take Alice to the prom. Circumstance had decided the matter for him. He trembled at the grotesqueness of thought without feeling. His mother was dying and . . . .

Davis checked himself. What was he assuming? Mechanically, logically, he began arguing with himself whether or not he had the right to make such an assumption. He could feel physical pain behind his forehead and temples. It seemed that thoughts were moving so fast they were burning up their tracks. His head ached, his eyes were throbbing. He got up and put on his shoes and coat, like a man who cannot sleep because of a noise outside his window. These noisy thoughts kept him awake. He went to the smoking room and lit a cigarette. The fumes only added to his discomfort, but he did not stop smoking.

He noticed that the train was moving. It was rocking from side to side and lunging forward, gathering speed. The click-clacking of the rails seemed to come from within his head. He did not remember when the train had started. He had no watch.

A frowsy-headed brakeman looked at him through the green curtained door. A big-lipped negro porter asked him if he were sick. Davis shook his head and smoked on. He was not used to tobacco. It made his fingers shake and his hands sweat. The porter returned with an envelope containing aspirin grains. He told Davis they would put him to sleep. Davis took two and a cup of water. While the porter was there, the train stopped. It was Newark, he told Davis.

From the station platform Davis could hear raised voices. He put his nose to the pane and looked out. There was a crowd of men and women waiting to get on. They looked like a troupe of actors. A uniformed official was bawling "North Philadelphia, West Philadelphia, Wilmington, Baltimore and Washington" just as if it were midday.

Several of the new passengers came into the smoking room. They were loud and boisterous. One of them invited all to have a nightcap. They took turns drinking from his flask. Soon they went to bed.

Davis considered returning to his berth but made no move to do so. He lay on his side resting on one elbow and holding the cigarette in his other hand. After a while he was conscious of being asleep and of dreaming. He had dreams of being cold and uncomfortable, of listening to Alvin discourse on religion and death.

He awoke and found himself covered with a red blanket. His head still ached. He rolled over and half-dreamed again. Then he got up and put cold water on his face and head. It was still dark outside. He lay down.

He must have slept because when next he was conscious the train was standing in a station. He looked out. It was still dark. Davis went to the door of the car and hailed a big slovenly man with a lantern.

"What is this? Washington?"

"Baltimore."

Only one hour more. He washed his hands and face. His fingers smelt of tobacco. He scrubbed them, sat down and smoked some more. He noticed that it was the last cigarette in the package. Twenty in five hours.

It was fifteen minutes past six when he alighted at Washington.   He gave the porter a dollar bill, drank a cup of coffee, ate an apple and caught the six-thirty-two.   Another hour.   It was just light when he stepped off at Cranston.   Alvin met him and took him by the arm.

"Not too good, old man.   The doctor's there now."

Then the emotion that had been damming itself up all night, burst free.   He wept bitterly going out in the car.   Alvin did not try to comfort him.   They did the twelve miles in less than twenty minutes.

Davis opened the front door.   There was a yellow light burning in the hall.   He felt Alvin take his arm again and saw the doctor coming down the front stairs. Alvin stepped past and looked at the doctor who spread his hands and shook his head.   Davis heard Alvin say "Christ!" and he knew his mother was dead.

XXV

Alvin watched Davis go upstairs to join his father, then he sat down in the living room. The butler brought him a cup of coffee. They had both been there all night. Alvin sat on. At nine o'clock Dr. Peckam came down from above. Alvin did not rise when the elder man entered the living room. He hardly looked up as he said:

"How are Jackson and the boy?"

The little minister sighed wearily and seated himself. He too had spent a sleepless night.

"None too well, I'm afraid, especially the father. I've never seen a man so crushed."

Alvin shrugged his shoulders.

"Pretty good day's work for your God of love, isn't it, Doctor?"

The old man looked away.

"Please don't, Mr. Martin. It's hardly the time, do you think?"

Alvin did not answer and Dr. Peckam after a few minutes' silence went on.

"At times such as these I often wonder if I haven't spent my life on a great delusion. There's so little I can say, so little comfort I can give. It's hard enough, sir, without you rubbing it in."

"I'm sorry, Doctor. It was cruel of me. I'm not myself today."

"I know, Mr. Martin, I know perhaps more than you think I do. Well, I must go. The day has just started for me. I've got other houses of sorrow to visit this morning."

"Let Manuel bring you some coffee before you go, Doctor."

"You know, I sometimes think that God withdraws Himself from people when they need him most. Very seldom is religion much help in the first darkness of grief. On the cross, God's own Son lost faith for awhile. It's a fearful thought, sir, when a man's coming to the end of his life, to wonder if it hasn't been one big lie."

"If it has been a lie, Doctor, it's been a magnificent white one. I wish mine were half as noble and unselfish."

"Well," the tired little man swallowed the coffee hurriedly and dragged himself to his feet, "once you've put your hand to the plow there's no turning. If I had to live it all over I'm afraid I'd tell the same old story, and believe it, too. These periods of depression depend a great deal on the condition of the flesh. If I can get a good sleep tonight, I'll be sure of everything in the morning."

"Good-bye, Doctor Peckam, I don't know whether there's a God or not, but if there is He ought to be proud of men like you."

Alvin offered his hand and the minister took it. Manuel helped him into his shabby overcoat while Alvin held the door for him.

Mrs. Pettigrier died on January twenty-first and on the twenty-third she was laid under the snow. Davis, by his father's urgent wish returned to college three days later.

The evening of this same day Alvin sat on the sofa in his Whelan Street loft, looking very weary. Between his heels was a tin waste basket in which a small flame was burning. By his right hand was a tin box. He was taking old letters and loose papers from the box, reading them and dropping them into the basket. The flame spurted up gratefully at each offering.

Alvin suspended his occupation as he heard footsteps outside the door.   There was a knock—a masculine knock and Mr. Louis Davis entered.

"Hello, Louis, come in."

"Don't get up, Alvin. I apologize for coming here, but it's rather important."

"It's all right, Louis. As a matter of fact, I sort of expected you. Will you have a drink?"

"Thanks."

Alvin rose and went to the cupboard. He poured out two whiskies.

"Sorry all I have is plain water to go with it. And no ice."

"I'll have mine as is," said the visitor, taking the arm chair and moving it so as not to face Alvin who returned to the sofa. There was a pause, then Louis Davis said:

"What you doing?"

"Burning up a lot of old letters and some foolish verses I wrote myself. Didn't know I was a silent poet, did you?"

"No, but I remember you used to write some at college. Alvin, I've got a very difficult message for you."

"Maybe I can make it easier for you. It's from Jackson?"

"Yes, how did you know?"

"Just guessed it, that's all. I was afraid it would happen that way. It's a damn shame."

By the electric light over his head Alvin's face showed taut lines and furrows. He fingered the papers in the box and crossed his legs.

"Yes," he said in a well controlled voice, "I kept on writing, or trying to write, after I left college. I always thought some of them weren't so bad. Here's one you might like."

Mr. Davis moved uncomfortably at this strange digression, but did not speak. Alvin selected a loose sheet and read:

"I used to think, 'when I grow up
    I'll be a gallant knight
And ride a horse and always force
    The wicked to do right.'

I thought, 'As soon as I grow up
    I'll save from every scrape
The lovely girls that lustful churls
    Pursue to wrong and rape.'

And so I bought myself a horse,
    And made myself a lance,
And went about to ferret out
    Some ready-made romance.

But now my lance is warped and bent,
    My horse is bowed and staved,
And old and weak I bravely seek
    Some girl who would be saved."

Louis Davis grunted. He hardly followed the context. These lawyer fellows were too smart for him. He gulped down his whiskey and made a face.

Alvin held the sheet caressingly over the basket. The flame reached up for it as he said:

"I'm writing a book, too. I've been waiting to see how it would end. Now that I know, I can finish it off in no time."

"What's it about?"

Alvin laughed as he rose and gave his guest another drink.

"What's it about? Well, that's a pretty big order. Life, love and the pursuit of happiness, I suppose."

The man in the arm chair nodded. Personally, he admitted to himself, he didn't understand Alvin half the time, but it was always better to pretend that he did. Aloud he said:

"I see."

"Now, go on with your message, Louis."

"Before I get to that, Alvin, I want to say something on my own. You see I've known for years about—about you and Molly."

"Yes, she told me once you did."

"I remember when she first started going around with Jackson. I believe she met him at my wedding. Anyhow, I always said he wasn't the man for her. I told her to take you. She was entirely too flighty for him. I even tried to tell him—in a different way—but no use. He was wild about her."

"Who wasn't?" said Alvin softly.

"What I really wanted to say was in way of an apology—for her."

"What do you mean 'apology,' Louis?"

"Alvin, how do you suppose Jackson found out all about it?"

"Don't know. Don't even want to know."

"Listen, Alvin, she told him. She told him on her death-bed. That's why I owe you an apology. She did it out of spite, because for the last year or so she has hated you. She's been unfaithful to her husband and to her lover. She couldn't even let poor old Jackson live on in peace. She's ruined both your lives and the boy's, too, if he finds out. I think I've got a lot of apologies to make."

Alvin started to his feet and strode to the far end of the room.

"That's no way to talk, Louis. My God, man, she was dying! She must have been delirious."

"Nobody wants to believe it more than I do, Alvin. I hope to God she was. I tried to tell Jackson that she must have been, but he wouldn't listen. He swore she told him in perfectly cold blood. I don't see how she could have had the heart. Poor fellow, he'll never be any good the rest of his life. The doctor's afraid he'll have a stroke."

"All I know is that Tommie wouldn't, couldn't have done such a heartless thing in her right mind."

"Alvin, a jealous woman—"

"Shut up. If you can't think of decent things to say, kindly get out of here."

"I haven't delivered my message yet, you know."

Alvin still stood facing the wall farthest from the other man.

"Sorry, Louis," he said differently, "I didn't mean that. Take your time."

"Well, I couldn't persuade Jackson of anything. Finally, I practically had to admit what she told him was true. I gave it away by denying it too strenuously."

"Go on."

"Then he said he wanted me to do him a favor. It was to come to you as soon as Davis left and give you this message."

"Well, what's the message?"

"That Jackson wants satisfaction—in the old way."

Alvin came slowly back to the sofa and sat down.

"I can't say I'm surprised."

Louis Davis went on:

"I told him it was nonsense to talk of a duel in these days, but he said by rights he ought to come down and shoot you at sight. He said he was only giving you this chance because you were a gentleman. I never knew people like him were alive any more. Proud isn't the word for him, he's absolutely imperial."

"Did he seem very much cut up that it was I, Louis?"

"God, yes. He kept on saying, 'Alvin, Alvin' and shaking his head as if it hurt him to think about it. Then the next minute he stamps around the room calling you names. I was afraid he'd have a stroke then and there so I promised I'd come right down and see you. How he could even expect to fight I don't know.

He's shaking in every joint and couldn't point a pistol at the side of a barn."

Alvin examined the lines on the palm of his right hand. Half an hour ago he had looked weary, but now he was positively haggard.

"I thought he held up pretty well at the funeral, but I suppose that was all for the boy's benefit."

"Yes, Davis left at noon. I promised to deliver this message and I have. The rest is up to you, Alvin."

"As a matter of fact, Louis, I had planned to leave town tomorrow night, but now I can't."

"Can't? You mean you've *got* to leave and leave tonight."

"I have no choice, Louis. I've been challenged."

"My God, Alvin, if you get one of your heroic fits! This isn't the time for any of that nonsense."

"No nonsense about it. Jackson has a right to take a shot at me. Besides, I've got myself to think about. A man's honor is something, you know."

"Honor! It's nothing but downright selfishness. You're always looking for excitement and now you've got a chance for it you're willing to sacrifice an old man whom you've already practically killed."

"Louis, I've got no idea of firing at Jackson. I wouldn't mind at all if he killed me. As a matter of fact, I hope he does."

"I know you do. You'd be pleased to die such a thrilling death and in order to enjoy the pleasure you don't care who suffers. How about Jackson after he's killed you? How about Davis when he hears? And you call it honor? I think you're pretty late discovering your honor. Where has it been for the last ten years when you were eating Jackson's food and seducing his wife?"

"Ordinarily, Louis, I would get up and knock your head off. If there was any seducing she did it, not I.

No, I didn't mean to say that. We were in love, that's all."

"I don't care what you were in. You and Molly together have done a rotten trick. Molly's gone and, by God, it's up to you, if you've the feeblest spark of decency, to patch things up the best you can. God knows you can't do much—but to sit there and talk about honor at a time like this! Honestly, Alvin, I thought you were more of a man—and a gentleman."

Alvin sat motionless. The little muscles about his jaws were quivering. The tan skin over his cheek bones had deepened to dark mahogany.

"When does he want this meeting?"

"Tomorrow morning at seven, but Alvin, if you meet him at seven, you'll do it after you've met me at six. If all you want is a fight, I'll give you that."

"Don't be a fool, Louis. I'm not going to fight you."

"No, you want to fight an old man."

"That'll be about enough of that, Louis. You've said plenty and I'm not going to listen any more."

"I haven't said enough till I get you out of this town."

Alvin jumped up from the sofa so quickly that Mr. Davis started in alarm. Alvin picked up the waste basket and set it in a corner.

"Louis, nothing would give me more selfish pleasure than to meet you at six and Jackson at seven. But you're right. It's up to me to salvage whatever I can out of Jackson's wreck of a life. I always hoped to make my exit with a *beau geste*. Standing still and taking Jackson's bullet would have been heroic. But things like that never happen to me. I'll go to Baltimore tonight and Saturday I'll sail for Vera Cruz."

They heard the street door open and someone coming up the steps.

"That's Nick," said Alvin. "I'll send him round to the club to pack."

Mr. Louis Davis walked over and stared at the ashes in the waste basket. Alvin having instructed Nick, came and stood beside him. They were old friends and did not bother to apologize.

"Alvin, I have another message for you. My wife said to be sure to bring you home for dinner."

Alvin laughed. "If you haven't any objections, Louis, I'll accept that one."

The two friends had dinner together. They talked of their old days at Kingston and Cranston when they were young men and wild ones. Mrs. Davis listened and laughed. She said she had never heard half the truth about her husband's bachelor life, else she would never have married such a rounder. The men exchanged good-natured libel. Alvin was charming. His reminiscences smacked of affection and feeling that he had never before shown. Mr. Davis ordered up from the cellar a bottle of old wine he was saving to welcome an heir that had never come.

At ten o'clock they returned to the coach-house loft in Mr. Davis' car. Nick was there with three suit cases.

"Nick, I'm going on a long trip, so I might as well give you that brown suit of mine. You'd probably steal it anyhow while I'm away."

The old darky beamed at the privilege of being noticed. He chuckled and bowed himself into a corner. "Mist' Alvin" had been in a wretched humor for weeks. Nick was glad to see the return of his genuine gruffness.

"Now, you black rascal, you, can you sign your own name?"

Yes, Mist' Alvin, he could.

"Then let's see you do it on this line."

After Nick had painfully executed this business Alvin beckoned to Louis Davis who put his signature below. Alvin folded the paper and put it in an envelope. On the outside he wrote "Last Will and Testament of Alvin Martin."

"Now, Nick, put these two bags in Mr. Davis' car. Leave this one. I'll bring it down.

Nick descended. Alvin opened the remaining valise. He went to a drawer of his table and took out a rectangular object. On top of the neatly packed shirts he laid face downward a framed photograph of a woman who had wrecked two strong lives.

Then Louis Davis drove him to the station.

XXVI

Time, like a winter wind, blew on, making ruddy the cheeks of youth and brittle the bones of age. It is seventeen months since Davis Pettigrier had watched them bury his mother.

It is October of nineteen-twenty-five and he is a first year student at the State University Medical School. Last June he had graduated from Kingston with high honors in English.

Last July the committee in charge of the Griswold Scholarship in English Literature, had mailed him an application blank. Davis had not returned it.

Mr. Pettigrier some two weeks after his wife's death was stricken with a complete nervous break-down. For a month he lay in his brother-in-law's house, his mind dashing itself against the bars of its cage. White-capped nurses tiptoed in and out of his chamber, specialists consulted in the ante-room and anxious friends whispered in the halls. When finally the poor mad brain had been tethered and soothed and the doctors allowed Davis to enter the darkened room there was another man beneath the sheets. The man had a long, gaunt body and held bony, unsteady hands against his temples. When Davis looked at the face on the pillow he experienced one of those vivid impressions that expresses itself in color. Looking at that face he had a sensation of grayness, the grayness of ashes. It was not that the damp hair was gray, nor the steel-colored eyes were gray; it was that the total image called up by the sight was one that had no other name than grayness.

Another fortnight and Mr. Pettigrier sat on the

porch heavily bundled.   He kept his hands in his lap
as if he were ashamed that people should see them
tremble.   He spoke briefly that people should not notice
the hesitation in his voice.   The eyes that had been
tender and mellow were dull now and expressionless.

Often he seemed to have no idea of the sequence of
events.   He asked for Molly and spoke of Alvin, as if
he expected to sit down to his next meal with them.
He wept for Bobby and Nancy as though he had just
heard of their death.   But there were other times when
he seemed sanely and cruelly aware of everything.   At
these times he would stare straight ahead with dim eyes
that fairly radiated grayness.   He would clench his
trembling hands beneath the blankets and shift his
drooping shoulders, like a tired bull at the mercy of
the toreador trying to shake out the darts that were
fastened in his flesh.

After the crisis Davis had returned to college but
made weekly visits to Cranston.   Over these week-ends
he would sit on his uncle's porch beside the wheel-chair
and talk of carefully selected matters and events.   Mr.
Pettigrier always wanted to hear about his son's college
work and Davis saw to it that reports were both true
and flattering.   Mr. Pettigrier sometimes talked of
Davis' future and when he did it was always with the
assumption of a medical profession.   He told Davis in
short jerky sentences that it had once been his own
ambition to be a physician and that now he was happy
to know it was his son's.   Davis did not offer to correct him.   Junior year went slowly by.

During his senior year at Kingston Davis had again
been the room-mate of Tom Stevenson.   Johnson had
not returned to college for academic reasons.   In that
year Davis realized as he had never done before the
healing qualities of unpretentious friendships.   Tom,
Phil and Joe had, without making him uncomfortably
conscious of their effort, been psychic tonic to him.

They had gone to and from his room with bluff, affectionate ease. They had been what only male friends can be to a man and had been so with tenderness that was not sentimentality and unselfishness that was not display.

To say that Davis had enjoyed his last year at college is true in the same way that a tired runner enjoys those few moments when, flinging himself on the grass at the end of his race, he is able to regain his breath and spent strength. Davis had experienced that feeling of surprise which men often have at the elasticity of their own hearts. If any one had prophesied that so much grief was to come to him, Davis would have said that it was impossible to bear it. Now that it *had* come and he *had* borne it, the fact, though still incredible, was proved. It astonished him that he could think of and care for trivial matters. At first he had accused himself of shallowness. He felt that it was wrong to want to go hunting or skating now that his mother was dead and his father stricken. He was several months learning that life belongs to the living, that even in grief the body and mind will not allow themselves to be ignored. Having once yielded Davis found a sort of fierce pleasure in physical exercise and danger. As Phil said, it was "winding up the clock."

Next to the society of his friends, Davis found most relaxation in the hunting field. He was now the owner of Johnnie Walker and the little horse carried him across country with the speed and security of a high flying swallow. He had inherited the horse at the death of Alvin, for in March of that same tragic year there had come to Cranston a death certificate of Alvin Martin. It came from a small town in Mexico and was signed by a native official. Alvin's seal-ring accompanied the certificate.

When the executors of Alvin's estate had opened the will they found it dated the day of his departure. It was legally perfect and signed by two witnesses. There was little enough to be adjusted. Alvin had no real estate and he had closed his account at the bank, presumably taking a large sum of money with him. There remained only his horse, his library and a few personal effects. The first two items went to Davis and the latter mostly to Nick.

Had Davis had less on his mind at the time, he would have been more puzzled by Alvin's sudden disappearance. Alvin had written from Baltimore to say that he was setting off on a long shooting trip which (strangely enough, said Cranston) was to start in Mexico. When, a few weeks later, the news of Alvin's death came, Davis, in throes of distress over his father's condition, considered it only natural that people whom he loved should die. When it became possible for him to think calmly again, Davis numbered Alvin among the lost things of the past, his mother, Margie, and his home-life.

Cranston had received the news of Alvin's death with incredulity. Ladies at their bridge parties and men at the club talked widely of his strange flight and sudden death, pretending to know a great deal more than they cared to say. Once, several years later, a Cranstonian traveling in Algiers heard a lieutenant of the Foreign Legion speaking French with a southerner's accent. The officer was engaged in a lively argument with several of his fellows and was rebutting every opinion with contemptuous snorts. Another time an unknown horse and unknown rider led the field of the Aintree Grand National in sensational style for four miles and looked like sure winners until the last fence when the animal fell and broke its back. Pressmen sought the rider to make a scoop of his story, but he had disappeared after the race and could not be found. People who were at the fence where he fell said that he was rather older looking than one would expect, that he had a dropped shoulder and that he swore as they had never heard a man before. Of course Cranston tried to identify both these persons with its own prodigal son, although no definite proof ever came to hand.

But the name of Alvin Martin in Cranston became proverbial. People there still say of a lawyer that he was "as smart as old Alvin," or of a young rider that he sits a horse "like Alvin Martin."

Experience, grief and responsibility had in two years made a stalwart man of a puzzled, ineffectual boy. Cranston would not admit surprise. Blood would tell, it said, and the boy was a Pettigrier and a Davis. Some of the older people said that Davis was the very image of what his father had been thirty years ago, but there were others who laughed and hinted that it was not Pettigrier blood which gave him that new confidence and courage.

While Davis was at Kingston, Mr. Pettigrier stayed with his brother-in-law. The old man needed constant attention. He could not get out of bed or a chair without assistance. He was for a time subject to sudden attacks of faintness and once was found overturned in his wheel-chair with a gash on his forehead. Mr. and Mrs. Louis Davis were all kindness and concern, so much so that Jackson Pettigrier's hyper-sensitive pride was wounded. He felt himself a burden on them. He demanded to be taken to the club and left in care of Manuel. This, of course, they would not hear of. The compromise was that whenever Davis came home on a holiday of any length the Pettigrier house was reopened and father and son lived there together.

After his graduation they moved permanently into their old home. The old gentleman was not at his best here. There were too many memories—a letter of Molly's in the pocket of an old suit, her initials on the table linen, her name written in many books. How it was possible for Jackson Pettigrier to keep his festering secret from his son is a mystery that does him credit.

The photograph of Alvin that had always been on the mantlepiece in the library, was, due to the forethought of Mr. Louis Davis, no longer there. There was another in Davis' bedroom, but that was not disturbed. Davis seldom introduced the names of his mother or of Alvin for fear of distressing his father.

During the summer that proceeded his entrance into medical school, Davis gave practically all his time and thought to Mr. Pettigrier. Twelve years ago the father had led the son. Now it was the son who led. The specialist from Johns Hopkins who had charge of the case said that the best and only cure would be some way to keep the patient from thinking.

"Introspection" he said, scarcely believing that anyone would understand the word, "is the most insidious of human diseases. Don't let him think."

That was the problem: to keep him from thinking. Davis tried reading aloud to him, but soon discontinued the practice. Whether the father heard echoes in his son's voice or whether he was not capable of the necessary concentration, the result was that Davis often looked up from the page to see the thin lips quivering and the dull eyes moist.

It soon became apparent that when he read to himself Mr. Pettigrier was more at ease. The effort was enough to keep his mind on objective thoughts. Signs of improvement were forthcoming. He slept better and seemed to lose some of his morbid indifference.

The Baltimore doctor congratulated Davis on the success of his efforts, but cautioned him against the possible danger of an emotional upset which the reading of some type of book might bring.

Davis was hard put to it to keep up an adequate supply with this limitation. Mr. Pettigrier read five and six books a week. He would take without hesitation anything that his son offered him. He developed a childish delight in seeing how quickly he could finish a book and demand another. There was pathos in his simplicity which increased daily. His mind seemed a hungry maw, ready to accept whatever could be crammed into it.

Davis tried several methods to supply or alleviate the demand for reading matter. He tried the simple expedient of offering a book that Mr. Pettigrier had read. This earned him a look of pained reproach. He tried time-annihilating games such as solitaire, checkers and chess, but without success.

Finally, by mere accident, he happened upon a solution. He found that the daily newspapers were exactly what he had been looking for and he subscribed to the papers of a dozen near-by cities. Every morning they arrived, fresh and unopened and every evening Manuel burned them down behind the stable.

The pathetic humor of it cut Davis. To see this wreck of a man rattling his way through sheet after sheet—it was ironic. Davis often thought of what Alvin had said about physicians. "They don't save lives, they only postpone death." They were postponing the death of his father; they had not saved his life.

XXVII

The State University was thirty miles from Cranston. The Pettigriers' driveway met the main road about half way between the two points. Davis took a room at the boarding house in the university town where he kept his books and studied. He commuted daily.

He did not try to persuade himself that he cared for his work, but with the sturdy discipline life had taught him he was able to do it creditably. His whole course of studies was distasteful. He hated the closely printed, freely-illustrated textbooks; he despised the boring, diagramed lectures; but most of all he loathed with a loathing of disgust the laboratory work.

Somehow it seemed that he could never get used to seeing human bodies handled like so much putty. It sickened him. It depressed him. He could not understand the callousness of his colleagues. Some of them joked about the motionless things that once had been able to joke themselves. These students called the corpses "stiffs" and the morgue "Stiff Hall." Davis shuddered.

In the evening when he came home, Mr. Pettigrier always expected to hear all about the day's work. He would often read over Davis' books and lecture notes. The fact that his son was studying to be a doctor delighted Jackson Pettigrier. He boasted in broken syllables that the world would soon have a Pettigrier to be proud of.

The autumn passed and winter came in bashfully as if it were asking, "By your leave."

Davis found his time crammed with regularities. He allowed himself one day a week to hunt. Three or four other days he rode Johnnie Walker before breakfast. He saw little enough of his friends. Phil Parsons was at law school; Joe Watson had taken a job in New York; and Tom Stevenson was in Cranston selling bonds. Every Sunday Tom came out for dinner and usually spent the afternoon. This visit was practically Davis' only opportunity for young society.

A few weeks after Christmas Davis received a letter from his old teacher, Dr. Down, who wrote that he had just remembered that a very dear friend of his, Professor Frank Lough, was teaching at the State University. Dr. Down begged Davis to pay this man a visit.

> "Frank Lough, I have always considered to be one of the most brilliant and appreciative lovers of poetry. If he had been able to escape the nets of Hymen, he would have gone far, but years ago he married and I have hardly heard of him since. I have written him by this same mail, but do not wait for an invitation to call. He is very slovenly in all his ways. Go see him and I promise you, my dear boy, many a happy evening of the sort we used to enjoy together."

A few days later Davis hurried through a grisly task in the laboratory. At four-thirty he sought and found the home of Professor Lough. It was a sun-blistered little cottage crouching behind an uncouth hedge. It seemed to squat there as if hoping to find shelter from the sleety-wind that had followed in the new year.

Davis pushed the doorbell and waited. Nobody heeded him. He tried again and a third time. The bell was out of order. He knocked. There were voices inside, but none of them invited him in. He knocked again with vigor and noted a sudden cessation of the sounds within. There came a babble of whisperings, then just as he was about to turn away with irritation, the door was whisked open.

A boy of fourteen with bristling red hair, unbuttoned collar and sagging trousers stood in the threshold.

"Is Professor Lough in?"

The boy turned his back, cupped one hand around his mouth and yelled:

"Hey, Pop, 'nother one of the guys to see you."

Then with no more ado he disappeared leaving the "nother guy" faced by an open door. Davis assumed that this must be intended as an invitation to enter, so scraping his feet hastily on the rubber mat, he did.

The professor's house, as if to establish immediately its informality, began brusquely with a small parlor fairly seething with disorder. One whole quarter of the rug was folded over. There sprawled a cluster of chairs in one corner and a table. On, about, and beneath the table swarmed children, representing, it seemed, all ages and genders. They had ceased their various activities and were staring at him.

Davis repeated his inquiry.

"Yes," said a ten-year-old, "he's here."

The visitor made a cursory search of the room. Save for a pipe which had spilt its ashes on the table top, he could find no trace of an adult person.

Then an inner door opened letting in a stream of culinary odors and a man. Davis realized immediately that the man must be the owner of the squatting little house. Indeed it seemed almost as if the man might have built the house to fit around his own body, he was of such squatting stature himself.

"Professor Lough?"

"Ah, good evening, Mr.—ah, yes. Good evening. What can I do for you? Let's see. Have you read your *Areopagitica?* That's very important. There hasn't been an examination paper for years without a question on Milton's prose. Have you read it?"

"No, sir, but—"

"Well, well. You must read it. I'm not saying it's on the paper, mind you, although I ought to know since I made it out myself. A very fair paper, perfectly fair, but you've got to read the *Aeropagitica.*"

"My name is Pettigrier, sir. I—"

"To be sure, I always get you mixed up with that man who sits next you in class. What's his name?"

"Professor Lough, you've mixed me up with one of your pupils. I'm not in your class, sir. I'm a friend of Dr. Down's at Kingston. He said he'd written you about me."

Professor Lough became even more gracious. He invited Davis into the dining-room where they could talk more quietly.

"Of course I remember you now. Old George Down wrote about you. Well, Mr. Perkins, any friend of George's is a friend of mine."

There was a new commotion in the living-room. A splintering crash and the wailing of a child. Davis started to his feet, but the professor sat unruffled.

"There goes the table again. Now, sir, tell me about old George. I almost forgot he was alive till I got his letter. The old scoundrel's still with us, is he?"

Davis told him about Dr. Down, stressing that their intimacy had begun over books. He mentioned the pleasant evenings they had spent together reading poetry.

"Ah," sighed the professor, "those are the things I miss. I don't suppose I've had time to spend such an evening since I was married. But I will find time. You must come to dinner some night, Mr.—surely, come to dinner. After the kids are in bed, we'll have a night of it."

"I'd love to, sir. Are these all your children?"

"Most of them, five, no, six of them. Six not counting Natalie. And then my wife makes seven, although
naturally she's not really a child—but that makes
seven. Eight, counting Natalie."

"And Natalie is—?"

"Yes, Natalie's eight.

There was another crash in the adjoining room.
Fresh screams. A beating on the floor. Davis looked
at his complacent host with amazement. That person
had clasped his hands behind his unusual little head and
was gazing with reminiscent revery at the ceiling. He
was speaking, but Davis, due to the clamor, could not
understand a word.

Suddenly the noise subsided as magically as the rebuked waves of Galilee and Davis caught the last part
of the speech:

"I don't know. I don't know. George Down has
his freedom and leisure, but I believe I prefer my cap-
tivity. There's nothing like a quiet family life for a
man's contentment. Get married young, I say. I
always tell Natalie to get married young. Hello, here
she is. Natalie, this is Mr. Young."

"Pettigrier," corrected Davis and rose.

Natalie Lough was dressed in a dark overcoat, and
galoshes. She had her father's tendency to squattiness,
but it seemed to go well with her big sensible face and
practical brown eyes. She greeted Davis without
embarrassment and leaning over kissed her father on
his head. She spoke in a voice that was as brown and
practical as her eyes.

"Daddy dear, every time I go out those kids tear
the house down. Can't you make them behave? I
should think they would drive you mad. Please sit
down, Mr. Pettigrier. I've got to set the table, but I
won't disturb you."

There was a half-hearted uprising in the living-room
which Natalie quelled by a quick sally. She returned

followed by a thin woman whose colorless lips were drawn off her teeth with canine ferocity.

Either unaware or unheedful of a stranger's presence she lunged at the recumbent professor.

"Frank, it's getting so I can't step out of the house a minute and leave you with the children. It seems to me after all these years that you could be some help. They've broken the table again and—"

"Mother, this is Mr. Pettigrier."

Mrs. Lough whirled on Davis and the canine snarl melted simultaneously into a feline purr.

Davis soon took his departure, going through the devastated area of the parlor and repeating his promise to call again as he stepped out into the sleeting world.

The fifteen-mile drive home that Davis executed five times a week was always an occasion for a deal of thinking. Usually it was of a depressing nature, for coming directly from the laboratory his spiritual lungs were filled with stale poison. There had been enough unpleasantness in his past to afford him much material for unpleasant reveries. And if it were not the past over which he brooded it was the future. What had he to look forward to? He had no goal. His life from now on was nothing but existence. He hoped to keep his father's body breathing for a while, that was all. For that he would drive every day to and from the university, going through the motions of doing work that sickened him. Five mornings a week he would drive fifteen miles to boredom and revulsion; seven nights a week he would return to a home where there was no home life, no contentment, not even relaxation. One day of seven was his own, his own and Johnnie Walker's, but the hours and thoughts that separated the returning of that day were innumerable.

He would recall sometimes his days at Barclay School. That was before the world had made him

think.   They were days when life was really what
people expected life to be—it had never been so since.
Life after that had been a biting dog that never
barked.

Sometimes it was of the opportunities for enjoyment
he had wasted at Kingston that he thought.   More
often it was of Margie and how by loving too much he
had lost what he loved.   The two words that recurred
again and again in these ponderings were "love" and
"life."   Davis wondered quizically whether love
spoiled life or life spoiled love.   Alvin used to say—
" 'Tis better to have lived and loved than never to
have lived at all."   Davis was not sure of it.

Davis visited Professor Lough again within the next
few days.   Soon after that he went to dine there, having left his father to spend the day and night with
Louis Davis.   He sat next to Natalie at table and after
dinner when he and the professor secluded themselves
with a stack of books, Davis missed her company, for
all the poetry they read.

XXVIII

Spring came early to Cranston. All things rejoiced.
The doctors told Davis that there was a slight improvement in Mr. Pettigrier. His pulse was slower. He
even tottered a bit sprightlier.

The drives to and from the university were done in
the light now and often he returned home in time to
play Tom a set or two of tennis.

He had learned how to accomplish his work with
the least possible effort and took an artisan's joy in
writing essays and reports, padded with second-hand
knowledge.

He was training Johnnie Walker for the Madingly
races on Easter Monday. People said he was fool-
hardy and heartless to ask so old a horse to race again.
They said Johnnie Walker had been a good enough
horse in his day, but that day had passed. They
prophesied quite openly that Davis would break his
own neck and kill his horse.

The owner of Johnnie Walker ignored these com-
ments. The fact was he wanted to ride so much that
he was able to persuade himself he was doing a perfectly logical thing. He sent Johnnie Walker to Alvin's
old trainer and every morning in March and early
April went over before breakfast to watch and assist
the progress of conditioning.

A few days before the Madingly races, Davis
stopped at the Lough's on his way home. He did not
ring or knock now, but went straight into the chaotic
parlor.

"Well, Natalie, how about Monday. Can you get
off?"

Natalie transferred a child from her lap to the floor,

tucked a vagrant lock behind her ear and rose to meet him.

"Davis, I'd love to do it, you know that, but you see how things are in this house. If I left on Easter Monday with all the children out of school, there wouldn't be two sticks nailed together when I got home."

They went out on the unshorn lawn and sat down on a moldy wooden bench.

"Natalie, I think it's a shame the way you have to work. You run the whole household, don't you? You never have a moment of your own."

"Well, I don't do it for fun, you know. Sometimes I get mighty fed up with it all."

"Of course you do. Now you deserve a holiday and Monday is your chance. We'll have a great time."

"It would be thrilling, Davis. You and Johnnie Walker are certainly the sentimental favorites. Everyone wants you to win."

"Natalie, if you're there it'll be much easier to win."

Natalie laughed and discarded this last with a practical toss of her full chin.

"Where did you develop that line, Doctor Pettigrier?"

"It isn't a line. I mean it and I really won't ride as well if you're not there."

"I'll ask mother," she agreed.

"If you take my advice you'll ask your father. He'll understand you better. Let's both ask him."

They set out early Monday morning because Davis wanted to walk the course before the race. Walking with Natalie he found it just as alarming as when he had five years ago with Alvin. He realized now what Alvin had meant by saying that half the joy of racing was being frightened beforehand. Davis felt thrills

of fear as he climbed over the big fences, knowing
that the next time he came to them they would look
even bigger. His study of biology had given him a
new reverence for living flesh. He had always reveled
in physical activity with unconscious, unknowing
enthusiasm, but now he felt that he appreciated it from
an aesthetic point of view. He felt that he would
enjoy the race with the same powers that made it possible for him to appreciate poetry. Poetry and racing
—it was life, concentrated life. He tried to explain
his feelings to Natalie as they were eating sandwiches
in the car.

An hour before the appointed time Davis found her
a place where she could best see the race and left her.
He dressed and weighed. Johnnie Walker had arrived
by this time. A negro groom was leading him around
the paddock.

Davis climbed up on the paddock fence to wait.
Most of the other entries were walking, too. It would
be a good field that started. There were three or four
young cracks whose names were beginning to be
known: Irish Dragoon, Micawber and the gray Pinafore all looked very fit and had many backers, but the
class of the field was Buccaneer, a big bright chestnut,
that a Long Island millionaire had sent down to win in
the South. To make Buccaneer all the more invincible
he was to be ridden by Dan Baker. "Skyline," as the
papers called him, had since Alvin's disappearance, no
rival to the claim of being the best amateur rider in
the vicinity.

Dan Baker joined Davis on the fence and showed
him how to rub rosin into the knee grip of his white
breeches.

"Dan, they tell me we aren't even going to see
which way Buccaneer went after he starts."

"Well, I ain't saying he's going to win this race, but
the horse that beats him will have to run like hell."

Davis tried to appear nonchalant in the presence of this celebrity, but he was jumpy with nervousness. He wondered if men who rode races ever got used to that last half hour of waiting.

Having dressed, weighed and saddled, the last preliminary details were accomplished. There was nothing to do but wait. In those last few minutes there came to Davis blank misgivings. What could have been more absurd than to enter an old horse in a high-class race such as this? Johnnie Walker would surely be badly beaten, his grand career would be ruined by an anti-climax. He could never go the pace of those strong young horses. They would run him off his feet and throw him down over one of the big fences. Davis gulped down silent remorse. If he were hurt it would affect his father badly. The doctors had said that any sudden shock—

"All up," called the starter.

They paraded to the post. Bucaneer was slouching along quietly, disdaining to show his nerves. He had won races on Long Island. There was Yankee arrogance in his carriage and mien.

Johnnie Walker was squirming. It had been a long time since he had seen those big shining fences with the red and white flags and the lane of human faces down to the post. He strutted with pride and excitement, and the crowd about scattered as his bright shoes flashed in a nervous buck.

At the start Davis found himself well-collected. He remembered his experience of being left in his first race. With the wisdom of a veteran jockey he swore back at the starter.

He was off with the first flight, and over the first fence in fourth place. Ahead were two horses he did not know and the gray Pinafore. Going across the next field Pinafore put five lengths between himself and the second horse. Davis looked around for Buc-

caneer. He had planned to take his pace from Dan
Baker. He found him on his left flank.

Johnnie Walker was running easily. He was always
nervous going to the post, but once a race started he
responded without resistance to his rider's will. They
moved on in that order for five fences. The gray horse
still romped out in front, increasing his lead steadily.

Pinafore's performance worried Davis. The gray
was commanding a lead of twenty or thirty lengths and
the race was well along. He looked back at Baker for
reassurance. Dan seemed undisturbed.

The tenth fence was the biggest of all. Johnnie
Walker arched over it like a cat. Almost half way
around, Davis thought, and the gray horse still going
strong. In another half mile the lead would be unsur-
passable. Again he looked at Baker and still Dan
seemed perfectly satisfied.

Davis was bewildered. Surely Dan would not lay
back and let Pinafore go unchallenged. Dan was supposed to be a wizard at judging pace. He ought to
know, thought Davis. But when they crossed the
eleventh fence and Bucaneer still hung back, Davis
decided to ride his own race. He called on Johnnie
Walker and went out to catch the flying pace-maker.

Johnnie Walker answered the call emphatically. He
flung his brittle old limbs down the grassy slope into
the twelfth fence and jumped it in his stride. He
caught the third horse, a springy black, who once
caught refused to be shaken off. Johnnie Walker and
the black ran as match race for two fields. They ran
too fast to jump well, and hit both fences hard, which
took a great deal of strength out of them both. At the
fifteenth fence the black horse fell and Davis saw the
rider get up hugging a broken shoulder.

The black horse was out, but there were two more
ahead. The effort had cost Johnnie Walker much
Davis felt him less buoyant as he urged him on. The

tired son of Red Label summoned what was left of his spent stamina. He ran up to the second horse, a bay, passed him with a straining of lungs and muscles, and with the breath steaming in his nostrils began to run down the fleet Pinafore.

Two more fields of grass and running, two more treacherous fences that defied clean jumping at such a pace. Johnnie Walker banged his way over them and winced from his swollen knees. Pinafore's rider turned back a defeated glance and went to the whip. The gray rocked in his stride. For a while he drew away from the pursuer, then he held his own, then Johnnie Walker passed him a staggering rush. Pinafore dropped back. He was beaten.

Only four more fences, Davis breathed, and about three-quarters of a mile in distance. He was well pleased with himself. Just at the right time he had moved up, challenged and beaten the field. The black horse was down, the bay and the gray were exhausted. He and Johnnie Walker could coast home now, and laugh at the people who had laughed at them.

His heart went out to the heroic little animal. It was a gallant run he had made, beating three different horses in individual engagements. He had outrun, out-jumped a field of over twenty. Davis wished Alvin were there to see him.

Johnnie Walker was weary and blown. He scrambled over his fences regardless of form, intent only on keeping on his feet until the winning post flicked past the corner of his eye.

Three more fences, half a mile. Davis wondered complacently where Buccaneer had disappeared. He smiled as he thought how he had outridden, or at least outwitted, the great Skyline. Dan was probably back somewhere in the ruck running his horse's heart out, trying to make up his ground too late.

Davis looked back. Pinafore was floundering badly.

Two other horses had closed on the gray.   Behind these three were several others unrecognizable.

Suddenly out of the crowd burst a lanky chestnut. Behind the ears of the chestnut Davis caught a white glimpse of set teeth.   It was Dan Baker on Buccaneer. Skyline was making his run.

Davis turned his attention to his own horse.   He took quick account of Johnnie Walker's condition and the remaining distance.   He reached for the whip in his boot.   All his self-satisfaction was gone now.   He cursed himself for a fool.   It was he, not Baker, who had broken his horse's heart.   He had chased the three front runners, raced them individually and tired his horse early in the course.   Dan had waited and the leaders had come back to him.   Now Dan was coming up beside him on a fresh horse and Johnnie Walker was fairly fumbling at the ground with his fore feet.

Red flashed on the left.   Buccaneer, exalting in his young and unused strength, was bounding along joyfully.   Desperately and together they charged the next fence.

Buccaneer jumped eighteen inches over it in high spirits.   Johnnie Walker broke the top rail, stumbled, staggered and went on.

Buccaneer took the lead by half a length.   Baker did not attempt to open up a distance.   He seemed satisfied to rest his horse a little for the long hill ahead.

They were both over the next to last jump.   Now came the test, the long, heart-breaking grade that led to the last fence and the homestretch.   The chestnut ran at it with the gladness of being fit, young and victorious.   Johnnie Walker's breath came in great sobs.   His muscles rolled and knotted under the lathered hide.   He pushed his nose up to Buccaneer's girth and there he kept it although Dan Baker was hand-riding furiously now, with the intention of coming to the last fence with a safe lead.

They swung into the jump. Davis remembered that Alvin had told him once how to save an infinitesimal moment by smashing through a last fence while others played safe by jumping it. He could not gain by running. His only chance was to drive through the top rail. There was everything to gain, nothing to lose. If he fell, at least it would be a glorious defeat, the kind Alvin would have loved. He took Johnnie Walker by the head and hurled him against the fence.

There was a splintering of wood, a sickening lunge. He was in the stretch and Dan Baker's stirrup clicked on his own as they pounded on to the finish.

Davis measured the distance. Thirty lengths, twenty, ten, five. His whip cut down once, twice. The little horse plunged with a new effort, and then people were shouting that Johnnie Walker had done it again.

XXIX

The Sunday morning after the Madingly races, Davis drove up to the squatting house of Professor Lough. He had come to take Natalie to his own home for dinner. She was ready and waiting for him, a thing he began to notice was not unusual with her.

"How's the hero?" she asked as he handed her into the front seat.

"Looking as if he'd like to run again next week. I don't see how he did it yet, but as Alvin Martin used to say, 'A horse that won't be beat, can't be beat.' That's the only explanation."

"Davis, I'm going to feel so embarrassed at your house. It will look as though I'm being put on exhibition for your father's approval. People won't understand that we're only friends."

She pulled her blue print skirt snuggly over her knees.

At his own driveway Davis suggested that they go down to the stable and see Johnnie Walker before dinner.

Johnnie Walker turned with a rustling of clean yellow straw to face his visitors as they opened the door of his box. He put his velvety nose into their hands hoping to find sugar. Davis recited the fine points with an owner's pride.

"Look at that head and eye. And the long shoulder and straight hind legs. Isn't he a grand sight? Never took a lame step in his life. Feel his tendons."

Natalie gingerly fingered the neat legs, but returned immediately to the less perilous occupation of stroking the mahogany neck.

"Damn that stable boy," Davis exclaimed without preface.

He took the water bucket from its wire hook in the corner of the stall and went out.

There was a splashing of water on tin and then water on water. Davis returned with a full bucket and put it on the floor of the stall.

"Hot day like this and no water. Wait till I see that boy."

Johnnie Walker lowered his head to drink, but as he was about to plunge his nose into the cool, clear water, there came from his nostrils a stream of hot, clotted blood.

Natalie saw it first and screamed. Davis stood horrified and said:

"Good God."

"Never mind about God. Get a sponge and wet it."

She took the sponge from him and held it to the streaming nostrils. Her dress was spotted with blood and water, but she did not notice.

"Get another bucket, Davis, don't stand there and watch me."

Davis, pale from the sight of blood, tried weakly to be of some use.

For fully three minutes the blood came, fell reeking and clotted on the yellow bedding. By that time the two human agents seemed to have Nature under control and Johnnie Walker stood with his forelegs apart and his nose against the matted straw.

"You'll make a fine doctor, you will," she taunted, turning to Davis who was leaning sickly against the wall. "Go up to the house and 'phone for a veterinary."

He obeyed running and returned running. Natalie was ruefully inspecting her bespotted clothing and hands.

"I don't know what I'm going to do, but I certainly can't come to dinner like this."

Davis was giving his whole attention to the horse who had not changed his position.

"Natalie, what do you think happened? Do you think he'll die?"

"Don't you ever come to my house when I'm sick. I never saw anyone so completely demoralized. And don't ask me questions. You're supposed to know something about things like that."

The veterinarian came in ten minutes. He listened to their account and made a brief examination of the stolid sufferer.

"Well, Mr. Pettigrier, I said to myself last Monday when I seen him run, that if that horse gets through without breaking down, then I don't know horses. You see, Mr. Pettigrier, a horse ain't like an automobile where you can put in a spare part and go on. Now this horse is getting along in years. I remember when Mr. Martin—"

"Yes, I remember all that, but what's wrong with him?"

"It's his heart, sir, that's what it is. His heart's gone back on him. Johnnie Walker has run and won his last race. Well, we all come to the end sometime."

"That's right, Doctor, but how about the horse. Can you do anything for him?"

"Oh yes, I could, but it wouldn't do much good. It would be plain suicide to race or even hunt him again."

"What I mean is will he die from loss of blood or anything right now?"

"Not likely, Mr. Pettigrier, but as long as he ain't going to be any good to you, the cheapest way is to let me destroy him. I'll come around in the morning. You can get five dollars for the meat at the kennels. That's about all he's worth now."

"I've got no idea of destroying him. You do what you can for him and I'll take care of the expense."

"Well, sir, some folks like to keep them alive and

that's their business. I'll give him some powders, but the main thing is a long rest. And, Mr. Pettigrier, don't ever gallop this horse or jump him over a fence, if you value your own life."

When the doctor had gone Natalie once again drew attention to her own appearance.

"Davis, I think you'd better take me home. I don't want to be seen looking like this."

But Davis would not hear of that.

"My aunt is coming to dinner. She'll do something about it."

Mrs. Louis Davis was at the house when they came in. She ordered her car to the front door and took Natalie with her on a tour of the neighborhood in search of clothes.

"If you put dinner back half an hour, I'll fix everything."

She did and Natalie sat down to table on Mr. Pettifrier's right looking none the worse for her borrowings.

Mr. Pettigrier sat at the head of his table with all his patriarchal pride. He held himself stiff and straight with apparent effort. He ate little and for the most part kept his hands in his lap. He turned to Natalie from time to time and spoke to her with his old-fashioned graciousness.

Natalie made herself charmingly attentive to him. She did most of the talking and appeared completely unconscious of his affliction. She conversed as if she were being entranced by the most accomplished of hosts.

Davis was aware of it all. He was pleasantly surprised that Natalie could display such *savoir faire*. He knew she was not of, what his mother would have called, the best families. This knowledge had been a check on his feelings ever since he had met her. Davis had been raised a snob and he had never outlived it. He instinctively wanted to know if a person newly

met was a "somebody." Natalie was not and her plain-
ness of feature and flatness of tone showed it. Yet she
was carrying off a situation in which gentility had
often painfully failed. He looked at his aunt and
uncle and found there the same wonder and admiration.

"By the way," said Mr. Davis, "where's Tom? I
thought he always dined here Sunday."

"Tom's up in New York, Uncle Louis. He's best
man for a friend of his, Bob Johnson."

"Friend of yours, too?"

"More or less. I knew the bride better though, Alice
Dupres. I met her on the boat going to Europe."

Davis took a strange pleasure in saying this before
Natalie. He saw her look at him as he mentioned the
name. He was glad when his uncle followed up the
subject.

"Probably an old flame of yours. I run into one
of mine every day or so. Great things, these old flames.
Wish I were young again. I'd light up a couple of
new ones."

Mrs. Davis turned sweetly to Natalie.

"You know, my dear, the man I married is the biggest braggart alive. I only married him out of pity
and ever since he's been boasting. I hope you'll marry
a man who has had real flames and not just imaginary
ones. Real ones are perfectly harmless but the
others—"

"Oh, I'm afraid I'll never have time to get married,
Mrs. Davis. I have a large enough family to run now,
without adding a husband."

They left the table and withdrew to the living-room.
Natalie sat down on the sofa and made a motion as
if she expected Mr. Pettigrier to sit beside her. Mr.
Pettigrier had since his breakdown never sat anywhere
in the room except in his straight backed chair, but as
he caught the significance of Natalie's motion, he gallantly crumpled his uncertain limbs on the sofa.

The other three exchanged knowing looks. They saw that Mr. Pettigrier had never been brighter and better since his stroke. Natalie seemed to evoke just the right amount of effort from him. He was exerting himself without undue nervousness. All three of them were thinking what a splendid thing it would be for Mr. Pettigrier if Davis were to bring Natalie Lough home as his bride, and while all three were thinking this, they were also thinking how impossible it would be for a Pettigrier to marry beneath himself.

XXX

If someone had stopped him that night as he returned from leaving Natalie and told him that a year
from then he would be a husband and a father, Davis
would not have emphatically denied it, although his
own opinion would have been to the contrary.

He therefore was not surprised when he awoke on
the third Sunday of April, 1927, in a bed of marriage
which was supplemented by a crib. It was a brilliant
spring morning, and if Davis Pettigrier had not known
better he would have been tempted to think that God
being in his Heaven all was right with the world.
Even little Jackie, his son and heir, seemed not to be
deceived by appearances. He was protesting already
against his thirty day confinement within the bars of
flesh. Davis was aware that this protest had been
the cause of his own return to consciousness. He
looked over his wife's shoulder at the crib, rose and
tip-toed around to the young agitator. He picked up
the baby and carried it, swaddled in clothes, out in the
hall to another door. Here he knocked and delivered
his burden into the arms of a nursemaid.

The clock on the bureau told him it was half-past six.
As noiselessly as possible he put on his breeches, boots
and sweater. The stable boy had not come yet so he
saddled Johnnie Walker himself. Cantering across
the meadow below his father's house Davis scoffed
at the dire predictions of people who said that Johnnie
Walker was unsafe to ride. They said that at any
moment his heart might stop and he would pitch end
over end. Davis headed for a low fence. Johnnie

Walker ambled into it and hunched over with complacent ease.

Ahead stretched a long green-grassy field sloping
downward. Johnnie Walker rattled the bit between
his teeth and lengthened his stride. It was his favorite
place for a gallop. Davis stood up in his stirrups and
crouched jockey-fashion over the wind-tangled mane.
Down the hill they rolled, going faster and faster as
Johnnie Walker's blood caught the tinge of April.
There had been few Aprils in his long life when he had
not faced the starter's flag. Today he felt as he used
to feel on April mornings years ago.

There was a brook at the bottom of the hill. It
had steep and rocky banks, but it was only ten feet
across. Johnnie Walker cleared it with a splashing
of pebbles as he landed. Beyond the brook was a loose-
ly built stone wall not three feet high. This usually
marked the end of the gallop for after this the ground
sloped up. Johnnie Walker left the ground a full length
too soon in his April vigor. His back feet kicked off
a few loose stones and he landed awkwardly with his
head down. He quickly regained his balance and pulled
up rather shamefaced, thought Davis, for misjudging
a take-off at this time of his life.

Davis let his horse walk for a quarter of an hour.
It was excitement enough just to breathe and look
and listen these mornings. He spoke to several farmers
that he met. They all knew him and smiled or spoke
with respectful familiarity. Davis made a five mile
circle around his house. He looked at his wrist watch
and clicked Johnnie Walker into a trot.

A cold shower and a rough towel sent Davis down
to breakfast ruddy and shining. He kissed his wife
on the forehead and touched his father's shoulder by
way of greeting as he sat down.

"Davis," she said, pouring his coffee, "I don't suppose there's any use of my asking again, but I do wish you'd get another horse to ride."

"Can't get another Johnnie Walker. Anyhow, it's perfect nonsense about his heart. Just because he had a nose bleed once, every one thinks it's his heart. I wish I'd raced him this year instead of listening to you-all. Maybe I will in the fall."

Mr. Pettigrier could not follow conversation at that speed. He saw only that his son was radiantly happy and that his new daughter was in one of her pretty pouts. Mr. Pettigrier felt unusually well this morning. In fact he felt well enough to go to church and sit between the children in the family pew.

Natalie Pettigrier was on the point of differing with her father-in-law's proposal to accompany them to church. There was company coming to dinner and Mr. Pettigrier would need all his vitality before the long day was over. She was about to voice her opinion, when Davis' frown checked her. He told her in an undertone it would do the old gentleman good to feel himself a member of society once more.

It had been several years since Trinity Church congregation had seen three Pettigriers file down the aisle to their pew in the third row. It caused a mild ripple over the smooth surface of the congregation. An observant person might have noticed that the surface had undergone a similar disturbance before the Pettigriers' arrival and that the aggregate result almost deserved the title of a very small wave.

Davis Pettigrier was pleasantly aware that their entrance had been noticed. He bowed his head as he entered the pew and tried to pray, but he was too well and happy to need heavenly aid. The choir came out of the vestry-room singing the processional hymn. Davis found the number and joined in:

"Guard us, guide us, keep us, feed us,
  For we have no help but Thee."

He remembered having heard Alvin use these very lines
to indict church-goers for fawning cowardice.

Dr. Peckam began:

"Dearly beloved brethren the scripture moveth us
in sundry places—"

Davis was fumbling for the book-rack to replace the
hymnal and in doing so he turned his eyes diagonally
downward.

Was it possible? Was he victim of a hallucination,
of some mystic reopening of the past? Or was it only
one of those illogical pranks that Fate delighted to
perform on never-learning mortals?

In the pew diagonally opposite his own stood Margie
Lucas, demure as ever, between her father and mother.

"Wherefore," pled Dr. Peckam, increasing the speed
of his delivery as he went on, "wherefore, I pray and
beseech you as many as are here present to accompany
me with a pure heart and humble voice unto the throne
of the heavenly grace."

The congregation accompanied him as far as the
floor of the church. Davis knelt mechanically with
them. He opened one eye and rolled his head just
enough to see over his elbow and into the pew diagonally opposite.

"Saying—Almighty and Most Merciful Father, we
have erred and strayed from Thy ways like lost
sheep—"

She had not changed, not a bit. He could see the
brown wispy hair sticking out from under her broad-
brimmed picture hat, the tiny, doll-like shoulders, and
—he saw it as she moved her head—the irresistible
pug nose.

XXXI

There were several guests at dinner. Tom Stevenson, shaggy-headed, and tending toward corpulence, sat beside Natalie who occupied the foot of the table opposite Mr. Pettigrier.

"Dave, remember Margie Lucas we used to go see every Sunday? She's back home."

"Is she? Oh, yes, I believe I did see her coming out of church. I didn't realize who it was till you mentioned her name."

Mrs. Louis Davis across the table smiled.

"To think that you could ever forget Margie Lucas. Why you used to eat, sleep and think nothing but Margie. Natalie, now that proves my theory. Louis never stops talking about his imaginary flames and Davis here says he forgets his real ones."

"I don't believe I ever knew her. Is she attractive?"

"Attractive?" echoed Tom. "Ask Dave."

"I haven't seen her for years," Davis evaded. "She used to be. Why isn't her husband with her?"

"Who said he isn't?" asked Natalie.

Tom prodded Davis with his elbow.

"She's got you there, Dave."

"Well," said Mrs. Davis, "he's not with her. She's divorced him and come to live here with her parents, bringing a good alimony along."

Soon after dinner Davis and Tom went off to play tennis. It was five o'clock when Davis returned home and all the guests were gone. He found Natalie in the nursery.

"Father taking a nap?"

She nodded. Davis leaned down and kissed her.

"What you so down about, Natalie?"

"Nothing that I know of."

Davis went to the shower. He came to her again, dressed.

"Natalie, I wish you were more cheerful. I want to tell you that you've been everything to me. You've really saved father's life and you've given me something to work for. I won't even mind being a doctor now. I know there's something that's worrying you. Please tell me."

He sat on the arm of her chair.

"Davis, did you like this Margie very much?"

"Oh, Natalie, what a foolish question. I knew Margie when she was fifteen and she was the only pretty girl around. Everybody had a case of puppy love for her. I suppose I did too, but what of it? Didn't you ever have a puppy love?

"Not really, Davis. I never had time. I always had to help keep house."

"Well, if you had, you'd know what a silly thing it is. All kids have it, just like measles. It won't be long before Jackie will think he's in love."

"All right, Davis, I didn't mean to be foolish, but your aunt talks so much and one does hear things around town. It's just as well I told you, though."

"Natalie, some evening we'll call on the Lucases and you'll be convinced when you see us together. We owe them a call anyhow."

"No, you go. I don't care to. Go tonight if you want."

"That might be a good idea. I could go now and wouldn't have to stay long. I'll say I have to come right home to supper."

Davis slid under the wheel of his roadster and drove off with a grinding of gravel. Sunday evening and going to see Margie! When was the last time he had done it? He thought back. In the Christmas vacation of sophomore year, over four years ago. Four years in time and how long in experience? Since then his mother had died, Alvin had died, his father had changed, Margie was a wife and he was a husband. He was going to see Margie again, but not Margie Lucas. Her name had changed, her home had changed. He had changed himself.

Davis drove to town by the short cut that he and Tom had used long before they went to college. For the sake of old sentiment, he decided to drive past her former home. He slowed down as he passed it and looked up the steps to the front door. He remembered the night he had kissed her hand standing there. He visualized the space beyond the door. The hall where he used to stand, hat in hand, waiting for her to come downstairs. The living-room where Sundays of five, six and seven years ago, she used to hold an open service of worship for her admirers.

He drove farther down town. The Lucases had an apartment in Ambler Hall.

The elevator man told him that Mr. and Mrs. Lucas were in. He ascended and knocked on the door. Mr. Lucas opened it. He did not recognize Davis. Davis was embarrassed to ask for Mrs. Schnell and, to make it worse, Mr. Lucas had grown deaf of late years.

As they were talking in the doorway, he heard a feminine rustling of clothes and the click of feminine heels within. Margie Schnell stood before him.

"Oh, Davis."

She brushed past her father and offered her hand. Davis remembered how it used to annoy him that his own hand was hot and moist when he took hers.

"Oh, Davis, how you've changed. You're so much older and bigger."

"And you, Margie, you haven't changed at all. You look every bit of eighteen."

They all three went into the living-room.   Mrs.
Lucas greeted Davis kindly.

"You're the young man who would never promise
to do any more than try.   What are you trying to do
now?"

"Trying to study medicine, Mrs. Lucas."

"That's wonderful, Davis.   You always wanted to
be a doctor, didn't you?"

"Yes, Margie—more or less."

Mr. and Mrs. Lucas excused themselves and left
the young people together.

"Margie, I'm married now and have a son."

"Then that was your wife with you in church.   She's
lovely, Davis.   I congratulate you."

She sat down in a chair and Davis chose to sit on
the window sill.

"Tell me about yourself, Margie."

He was almost positive that her lip quivered.   He
wished he had been more tactful.

"Myself?   Oh, there isn't much to tell.   Roswell
and I just didn't get along.   We didn't even speak each
other's language.   First we were only to separate,
but then he wanted to marry again, so we got a divorce.
That's all."

"Poor Margie, I'm sorry I asked.   It was stupid of
me."

"Not at all.   I don't mind talking about things—
to you.   Don't you remember that night in Paris?   I
wanted to tell you even then, but I didn't dare.   Don't
look so scared, Davis.   I'm not going to cry again."

"Since I've seen you my mother has died.   Alvin
Martin is dead too.

"I know."

"And, Margie, last year I won the same race on
Johnnie Walker that I did when you were there."

"You mean the time you carried my picture."

"And you wore a cape of my colors. Weren't we children?"

"Yes, weren't we."

They reminisced in low tones, reminding each other of incidents they had not thought of for years. The clock crept on unheeded until Mrs. Lucas came in and asked Davis to stay to supper. It was a quarter past seven.

Davis drove madly homeward. He was half an hour late and when he arrived he found his father in a bad state of nerves. Mr. Pettigrier did not look the same man that he had at dinner. That expression of grayness had returned to his countenance and his hands were very unsteady.

Davis blamed himself for his thoughtlessness. He should have known that any irregularity which suggested danger to himself would upset Mr. Pettigrier. If this had happened a year ago it might have had serious consequences. The doctors had warned him against undue excitement.

Thank heaven, now he had Natalie to share the responsibility with him. Her presence in the household had worked wonders. Natalie and Margie, his brain kept repeating as he lay in bed that night, Margie and Natalie, Margie and Margie.

XXXII

It was more than a coincidence that the early pedagogic fathers, when they organized the scholastic year, chose to make the examination period come in the first month of summer. These seers had in mind a symbolism with which to impress those they were preparing to meet the world. If they had merely lectured their pupils saying that the world is an undefinable enigma of good and bad, beauty and filth, joy and sorrow, they might have talked all day without the slightest results, but the method of forcing young minds to dull and certain unhappiness while Nature all around is green with joy, was effective. It was teaching life, instead of teaching about life.

"Six years of school, four of college, two of medicine, twelve years. Twelve Junes have found me like this."

Davis jammed his pencil into the crease of his notebook and broke the point. Taking the opportunity for an excuse to call a brief respite he left his desk, lighted a cigarette and strolled puffing about the murky little room that he used for a study.

"June," he mused. June the month of flowers and sun, of books and headaches, of moony nights and late-burning lights. Nature all unconscious of protoplasms, cells and microbes enjoyed them, while he, who was supposed to know all about them, was miserable. Nature was blissfully immortal, as one could plainly see by looking out of the window, yet he, a part of her, had to stay inside the window learning how to save her immortal life. Doctors lived, he thought, pressing his lips against the window-screen and blowing smoke, the most futile of lives. They work on a case of pneumonia, conquer it, only to have the patient carried off in a few years by another disease. No doctor had ever won a final argument with Nature, for no doctor had ever lived or made live forever. The Johns Hopkins specialist had gained professional fame for his brilliant work on Mr. Pettigrier's case. Yet at any moment Mr. Pettigrier might lapse back to his worst condition. He might die in bed any night from the slightest nervous disorder.

But if the medical life was one of futility, what life was not? What man of any calling ever won? If you competed, thought Davis, you lost and if you thought, you were baffled. It was better to busy one's self with living, rather than with thinking how to live longer, or how to inherit kingdoms in heaven.

The indolent little street below him was sticky with soft tarvia. A dog lolled along with exposed tongue. Beyond the houses across the street he could see meadows of goldenrod and frowsy dandelions. He wished he could canter Johnnie Walker through the field making the grasses go "swish" against his legs. That would be more sensible than sitting in this murky room learning diagrams of the digestive system.

A cream colored roadster came purring up the street. The lolling dog gave way. He could hear the tires crackling over the soft road and see their imprints in the road-bed. The car was coming very slowly. He thought the driver was looking at the numbers on the houses.

It stopped below his window and the driver stepped out. Davis murmured his astonishment and turning bolted out of his room down the steps to the front door.

"Margie, for heaven sake, what are you doing here?"

"Now, I wouldn't call that a hearty welcome for a lady paying an afternoon call. Especially when I had such a dreadful time finding your house."

Davis Pettigrier returned to the Medical School in October for his final year. He had not excelled in his work, but he had kept well up in the class. He had learned to make good use of his mind and memory. The results he had accomplished had been reached by careful selection of details and strict conservation of energy. He had not learned to like the work, but he had learned resignation to a more efficient degree than he had at Barclay School. He no longer looked on his future occupation with loathing. Being a doctor would not keep him from the library or the hunting field, he meant to be certain of that. As long as one had to go through the motions of being a useful citizen, Davis supposed one profession was really little better or worse than another.

His study-room was less murky this autumn. Some one had hung a few pictures on the wall, had installed a gramaphone and a tea set. These latter utensils were in use at the present moment.

"Turn it off, please, Davis. Have some more tea?"

Davis seated himself on a chair that was directly across the room from her.

"No, thanks. What worries me is how I'll ever get this essay in tomorrow morning."

"Are you trying to say it's time I went?"

"No, Margie. I wish you never had to go and you know it all too well. If you didn't you wouldn't be here. You shouldn't anyhow."

"Why not, Davis? I don't know anything more innocent than two friends having tea together. If we can get a little pleasure out of it I think we should. Lord knows neither of us have had the sweetest of lives."

"I don't suppose there's anything essentially wicked about it, but people would talk if they knew."

"Davis, you're getting so practical. Aren't you ever romantic as you used to be?"

"Margie, do you know what one of my ambitions used to be when I was romantic? It was that you should be the first and only girl I ever kissed. Even if you married someone else I wanted to kiss you at the wedding for the only kiss of my life. That was romantic, wasn't it?"

"Oh, to know that you felt that way about me and to think I married a man like Roswell Schnell! Davis, didn't you hate me?"

"The only time I nearly hated you was the night of the prom when Phil told me what he did. For awhile I felt there was nothing left in the world after that illusion was gone, but I got over it. We always do. I suppose the real reason I got so excited was that I was subconsciously jealous that others should get what I wanted."

"Davis, all you ever had to do was ask for it. I couldn't ask you, could I? That night you kissed my hand I was so disappointed."

"Disappointed? That was what I call one of my great white moments. It's you who aren't romantic."

She did not answer.

"Margie, the other day after you left I did something very foolish. I wrote something in the fly leaf of my biology book. Listen:

> Oh, where are the great white moments
>   When Margie and I would meet,
> And I was a worshipping heathen
>   Bowed down to the dust at her feet?
>
> Oh, then I was wretched and foolish,
>   And now I am wretched and wise,
> But where are the great white moments
>   I lived when I lived in her eyes.

"Davis, if I'd only known you felt that way, we might have been so happy together. Sometimes I think God goes out of His way to make trouble."

"Twice I've lost you Margie. If I'd known you were getting a divorce I would have waited. Natalie is a wonderful girl and she's been what nobody else could have been with father—but she isn't you."

"And Roswell is everything that you aren't, Davis, and nothing that you are. You'll never know the kind of people I had to meet out there and the way we lived. Why did I ever do such a thing? Now we can never be happy again, never, never, never."

Youth came to youth across the room in three long strides. He knelt beside her and took her hands. Her voice seemed to bubble up through a well of tears as she said something he did not understand. He did not care, because the next instant with his lips against hers he felt that he understood every mystery life could offer.

XXXIII

For the first time in his career as a student Davis Pettigrier regretted the coming of the Christmas vacation. It meant a temporary end to those afternoons with Margie. She begged him to call at her apartment but this he could not bring himself to do. They met not infrequently at social affairs, where they feigned an austere formality.

Three days after Christmas there was ice. Natalie did not skate, so that night after dinner Davis went off to the pond with Tom. Davis had not seen Margie to speak to for a week. He hoped she would come skating.

He put on his skates in the car and walked on the toe points across the frozen ground to the ice. The night and chillness thrilled him. He dug in his toes and with a running start began to race along the circumference of the crowded pond. He weaved in and out among the skaters hardly noticing them. He was looking for a slim figure which he would know without looking at the face. There was a bonfire on shore, making shifting shadows all about.

He circled the pond. Again he went around, slowly this time and peering at every one. He went ashore and tip-toed steel-shod to the fire. He went along the line of parked cars only to return disgruntled to the pond and the fire. For an hour he searched without success.

Tom came up to him.

"Come on, Dave, we're organizing a hockey game by fire light."

"Tom, I believe if you don't mind, I'll go home. I

don't like to leave Natalie alone. Can you get back all right if I take the car?"

Tom could and Davis drove homeward. Approaching his own driveway he slowed down. It was only half past nine. If he went home he would have to talk to Natalie for an hour or so. Of late he had shunned conversation with her. He dreaded lest she should ask some question or even mention a name that would make him feel uncomfortable. Instead of proceeding up the driveway, he backed out of it and went to town.

He felt sorry for Natalie. There was so very little that they had in common. She was never wholly at ease in Cranston society. Her friends were not his friends, nor his hers. Davis remembered Tom and mentally excepted him. Tom could be anybody's friend.

Still soliloquizing, Davis drove to Cranston and to Ambler Hall. He was there before he had planned what to do, so he drove around the block. His disappointment in not finding Margie at the pond made him reckless. Another turn of the block. He parked and boldly asked the elevator man if Mrs. Schnell was in. She was, and Mr. and Mrs. Lucas were out. Davis went up.

The next day it rained. It rained big, soft, melancholy drops, like a woman's tears. They thawed the frosted ground and warmed the dead grass in the fields. Against the window panes of the house that Jackson Pettigrier built, it came pattering.

Davis, son of Jackson, sat in his library with a book across his knees. The drops on the window panes made him want to read, but he could not. His mind would not go forward. Last night he had talked long and deeply to Margie. She had been a different Margie that night than he had ever known before. She had

been forceful, strong, insistent, and he had listened
to her although he did not like the subject.

Margie wanted him to take steps to free himself.
Happiness mattered, she had said, more than propriety.
Selfishness was inevitable. It was high time he acted.
He could not beg the question indefinitely. Last night
he had been almost convinced, but today he was hearing the other side of the matter within his own soul.
Blood, he was admitting, is thicker than water. There
were other and older bonds of his heart than those
that bound him to Margie.

At breakfast he had seen his father and wife sitting
at opposite ends of the table. It was Natalie who was
home with Mr. Pettigrier all day, whose tenderness,
thoughtfulness and care had brought the old man back
to something of life. Natalie had been in many ways
what Margie could never be capable of becoming.

Davis had resorted to procrastination. He had told
Margie that circumstance decided more matters than
men did, that men's proposals were very seldom considered in the final court of decision. Margie had not
cared for his theories. She said the time had come to
be practical and to act.

Mr. Pettigrier came into the room. Davis saw that
he wanted to talk. It was a rainy day, they said, a
good day for reading and talking.

Davis thought of the many times he and his father
had met in this room. Here of evenings years ago
Mr. Pettigrier had helped him with his lessons, holding him down to arithmetic and geography which the
boy had so despised. Here they had met in disciplinary
conferences and Davis had not forgotten the stout
hickory cane which used to stand in the corner behind
the door so that it was only seen when the door was
shut.

Upstairs Davis could hear the voice of the other
Jackson Pettigrier. There was another loyalty, he

thought. The old ones and the new. They were ever-present, ever-insistent. Besides he had given his word to Natalie at the altar of God. Margie had not considered this binding. She had said that he was free to decide. Davis was glad he was not.

After lunch he went down to the stable and fed Johnnie Walker some sugar. It was still raining. There was no chance of a ride today, but if the frost stayed out of the ground there would be good hunting soon. He ran his finger down the unblemished tendons. He had not told anyone that he had been thinking of trying Johnnie Walker in one more race this coming spring. It was reckless and foolish, he knew, but reckless and foolish things were invariably the most pleasant. He went back to the house and made himself read hard all afternoon.

Tom Stevenson came to dinner that evening. He was in a jubilant humor having sold two bonds during the afternoon. He laughed when Davis said that he had been reading all day.

"I read a book last year, but I forget the name. You ought to read it, Dave, it was good."

"What book are you reading this year, Tom?"

Natalie said it was a pity the rain had spoiled the ice.

"Damn shame," agreed Tom. "We had a great game last night. Sorry you have your husband so well trained that he wouldn't stay. Said he had to be home early."

Natalie emptied her water glass deliberately.

"Yes, it was early when I heard him come in."

She betrayed no irony in her countenance or voice, but Davis felt suddenly sick. Absent-minded, blundering old Tom. Well, it was done now. Circumstance was beginning to take things out of his hands already. He turned to his guest and said:

"I didn't know you sold bonds on rainy days. I thought you went to the Club and waited for the sun."

"That's where I was and what I was doing, when who should walk in but a customer. After a second high-ball I went after him. Then I won twelve dollars from him at bridge. I never could understand why people say this is a hard world. I think it's easy enough."

"Well, I suppose it's all in knowing how, Tom," said Natalie.

"Besides," Davis interjected, "you are blessed with wonderful talents, Tom. Men with your talents never have trouble with life."

Pensively Tom inserted a portion of hot potatoes into his mouth. He was not sure whether he was being teased or flattered.

After dinner they played cards. Mr. Pettigrier had only been able to resume card playing in the past two months and he still required a great deal of patience from his partner. Natalie sat opposite him tonight and proved herself supremely capable of the situation.

At ten Mr. Pettigrier retired and the game broke up. At ten-thirty Tom left. Davis turned from the door he had just closed behind his friend and saw Natalie putting the cards away. He walked up behind her and put his hands on her shoulders.

"Good night, Natalie."

"Wait a minute, Davis, I want to talk to you, if you don't mind."

"I'm awfully sleepy. Won't tomorrow do?"

"You shouldn't be sleepy. You came in early last night, didn't you?"

"About one, Natalie. And if you want to know anything, please don't bother to hint around."

"I wish I didn't know all I do, Davis. I'd much prefer to be blind to some things, but I'm not and I've got to see."

They seated themselves on the far ends of the sofa. Davis asked her what she saw.

"I see that your heart is somewhere else, Davis, than in your home. I'm not surprised about last night because it isn't the first time facts have come to hand. I needn't go into details, but I want you to know I haven't been spying."

"Natalie, I could explain it to you but you wouldn't understand. Would you believe me if I said I couldn't possibly help myself? Some powers are invincible."

"There was no invincible power that made you take me from my father's house and then break faith. Temptation is only pleasantly strong, not invincible, unless you want it to be."

"I've never been unfaithful, Natalie. Not that, I promise."

"Well, I'm not going to quibble over the word. What we must do is get down to business. I'm sure you can't expect me to stay here, so tomorrow I'm going home. I'll expect you to give me a divorce in the quietest way possible."

"Natalie, what are you talking about? You're wild. Of course, I won't give you a divorce. What do you think would happen to father?"

"Happen to father, Davis? You talk as if I were a paid nurse. You've treated me that way too. Don't you think anyone but a Pettigrier can have pride?"

"That isn't true. I've introduced you to my friends and made you one of the family. I think you'd better go to bed and calm down. We'll talk it over quietly in the morning."

"We'll talk it over right now, as quietly as you please. Don't think this is just a sudden fit of temper or jealousy. I know a lot more than you think I do. Did it ever occur to you that I have a mother living at the university and that she has friends? No, Davis, I've known what's going on and I was just waiting for the climax. Now it's come and it's time to do something about it."

"But, Natalie, please listen to me. Nothing like that will ever happen again. I give you my word. From now on we'll begin again."

"It's no good. We might as well be practical. Our marriage was a mistake. You're in love with someone else. I don't see any use going through with the farce. The sooner we set out to correct our error the better for all. I should think you would leap at the opportunity."

"I'm thinking particularly of my father, Natalie. You know perfectly well what the scandal will do to him. And you also know that he needs you. How could you do such a thing? Just think it over till tomorrow."

"I've thought it over, Davis. After all, you've yourself only to blame. I have a father who needs me. Even if I didn't, do you think I'd stay here under such circumstances? I have pride, too, if I must remind you again."

"I won't let you go. I won't give you a divorce."

"Won't you? Suppose I name a certain party as corespondent?"

"Oh, Natalie, you couldn't. Don't you know I've loved Margie all my life? Don't you know her name is sacred to me? If you'd ever loved, you'd understand."

"How do you know I'm not in love myself, Davis? You don't believe it's possible, do you? Your love is the only one in the world, isn't it, and the rest of humanity must stay at home and keep your house while you are loving."

"But you aren't in love or you would understand."

"Well, if I am at least I haven't been entertaining a lover in your absence or sneaking off to his house. I'm not a Pettigrier or a Davis, but my oath does seem to mean something more than yours does."

"Natalie, I've given you my name and you owe it

to those who made it mean something to keep it clean. There has never been a smirch on the name before, never a scandal for people to leer over. You wouldn't besmirch it now, would you, Natalie? You can have everything, even your lover if you'll stay."

"I ought to slap your face. So that's your honor, is it? You with a mistress and your wife with a lover, just so we keep up appearances the great name is clean. There's nothing more to say after that. Goodnight and goodbye. I'm really sorry for your father's sake, Davis. Tell him goodbye for me."

"Natalie, wait a minute. What am I to do? How can you leave me with no warning? You might at least help me a little."

She had risen and stood smoothing her dress with her hands. She turned her brown eyes on him with almost maternal indulgence.

"There isn't really anything I can do for you, Davis. I would if there were, but I honestly believe that the sooner I go the easier it will be. I hope this Margie person will be able to take care of you. Somebody will have to."

XXXIV

Davis had risen mechanically with Natalie. He watched her go out of the room, heard her heels clicking up the steps, heard her enter their room upstairs and lock the door. Then he sat down heavily on the sofa. As usual, he thought, circumstance had made the decision and he had to abide by it. It would be utterly impossible to keep the thing from his father. What the effect would be, he feared to think.

Crossing the room he took from a cupboard a package of cigarettes, sat down and smoked. If man were a rational animal, there would be no regret, no remorse, no suffering. It was plainly irrational to cry over spilt milk. Yet men always did. They had enough reason to see their own mistakes, but not enough to prevent them. Men were like moths flitting about a candle, capable of seeing the flame, incapable of avoiding it. Men were to Fate as flies to boys. They had their limbs pulled off and were left to live cirppled and shorn until a leisurely finger deigned to crush them.

And the publicity of it all! How Cranston would talk! What a wind-fall for the tea tables and club rooms! "Young Davis Pettigrier, Jackson's boy, and a divorced woman, daughter of Lucas, who ought to be in jail."

Margie, the sacred name, it would be on every foul tongue in town!

As he smoked he felt the creeping on of the dull, deadening headache which he remembered having had that night when he came down from Kingston to his mother's death-bed. He welcomed the discomfort.

237

It was a relief to shift some of the suffering to his physical being.

There were two Jackson Pettigriers in the house, both unaware of life at the moment. There was consolation for one in that the Leisurely Finger would probably crush him soon. For the other Davis shuddered. He would have liked to consign him to the care of that One who is said to temper the wind for the shorn lamb, but Davis remembered tonight that he had never had anything except heresay evidence as to the whereabouts of that One.

He smoked and thought. It was one o'clock. Charles of England had been a sinner and was beheaded. Christ of Nazareth had been a God and was crucified. Cæsar of Rome had been a murderer and became Emperor. Hannibal of Carthage had been a patriot and took hemlock. His mother had taken communion at the holy altar; Alvin had drunk gin at the Club. They were both dead.

Three o'clock. He went upstairs to the third floor where he had lived as a boy. His old room was desolate with abandoned disorder. He took off his coat and shoes and lay on the sheetless bed, blowing gray smoke into blackness.

Outside the window there were patterns in the sky. Planets moved about the suns making patterns. The whole universe moved tirelessly, inevitably, designedly.

Five o'clock. If the shock would kill his father outright, it would be more merciful. Six o'clock. He looked out of the window. There was only a suggestion of dawn in the east. In that direction was Margie. He put on his shoes, a sweater, a coat, went downstairs and out the front door. It was still drizzling warmly, but the air was cold. He went to the garage and brought out his car.

Over this road he had driven in all kinds of moods, in depression, elation, ambition, futility, anticipation

and remorse. He turned down the unfinished road that
cut across the railroad, stopping twenty yards from the
tracks.   It was six-thirty by his wrist watch.   The
morning mail train came by at six fifty-five.

There was nothing distinctive about death.   Everything that lived died. Big-cheeked babies, pink-cheeked
girls; strong men, weak men, brave men, cowards;
keen-eyed thoroughbreds, squalid cattle; violets, lillies,
dandelions—everything died.   Dying was no accomplishment.   It was the one thing that all men could
do with equal efficiency.   You could not be mediocre
about dying.

Death was an open door leading out.   There was no
reason, after all, for men to suffer.   The door was
always open.   If a man were a rational animal, there
would be no regret, no remorse, no suffering.

He sheltered a match between his palms and lighted
a cigarette.   Life was a pattern.   Until one's pattern
was finished one had no right to die.   Living was man's
business, not dying.

Here came the train.   Here came Death.   Snorting,
smoking along through the nascent dawn.

Davis dropped the cigarette, slipped his car into
gear and moved slowly forward.   Death came lunging
on, shouldering its way through the thick atmosphere
of a living world.

It burst around the curve which cut the road Davis
was on.   Huge, black, shapeless, throwing off sparks
like a big dog shaking its wet ears.   It thundered and
roared at him, wound steaming across his line of vision,
and was gone.   Death had passed by, unhailed.

Davis turned his car about and drove home.   Shud-
dering, he thought of the devastation that his death
would have caused; of his father, and of Margie, when
they tried to live on after the shock; of Natalie and
little Jackie.   Driving home with the cold logical wind
making him shiver, Davis knew that he had just missed

doing a tragically selfish thing. No matter how much Natalie's departure would inconveniece and embarrass, suicide would solve no problem but his own. Her leaving would be unpleasant but not irreparably so. He had exaggerated his father's dependence on her. Margie would more than take her place. In fact, as he approached home, he was on the point of convincing himself that Natalie's action would in the end benefit all. They would all start afresh with every right to hope for happiness.

When he arrived at his house it was fairly light. The rain had ceased to fall and had left the air moist and pithy, the ground soft. He helped the groom saddle Johnnie Walker and mounted, clad as he was in a tweed suit and sweater.

Out in the meadow below the house Johnnie Walker moved off into a springy trot. His feet sank squelching into the mud. Davis' back ached and his head was heavy. He breathed deeply and urged Johnnie Walker into a canter. Over the low fence, out of the meadow. Ahead sloping downward was the long stretch that in the summer was green. Now it was winter-colored. As Johnnie Walker gathered speed, Davis felt great gusts of exultation blowing through his soul, whisking away his bodily discomforts. It was better to meet Life here on the hill-side than Death by the railroad tracks. He assumed the crouching seat that he had learned from Alvin. Death could wait until he had finished riding horses and loving Margie.

Johnnie Walker was spinning down the hill at a racing clip. He, too, felt exultant this morning. Perhaps it was the breaking up of the frost by the warm rain that made him feel as if he were doing an April gallop, or perhaps his rider's young exuberance was contagious.

The brook was before him. He measured the distance and lengthened his stride. He put his forefeet on the far bank and then his head went down with a lurch. Davis felt and saw hot clotted blood spattering against his trouser legs. He pulled at the horse's mouth to stop him. Ahead was the low stone wall. Johnnie Walker took two short strides, then with a convulsive effort he lunged forward and down. For a fraction of a second Davis Pettigrier was riding the body of a dead horse; the next he lay still beneath it, with his head broken against the stone wall. The rain came falling again, warm upon his upturned cheek. The three grim sisters clipped their threads. They had done with the life-pattern of Davis Pettigrier.

THE END

www.ingramcontent.com/pod-product-compliance
Lightning Source LLC
Chambersburg PA
CBHW050514260626
47157CB00004B/1317